DANDELION

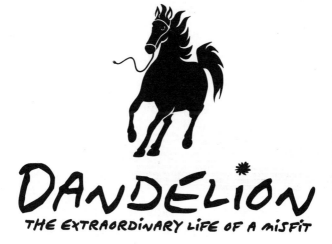

DANDELION

THE EXTRAORDINARY LIFE OF A MISFIT

SHEELAGH MAWE

TOTALLY UNIQUE THOUGHTS®
P.O. Box 2962 Windermere, Fl 34786-2962

Library of Congress Catalog Card Number

94-90296

ISBN 0-9642168-0-9

Printed in Canada

For
Calli and Sarah
with love

Also By Sheelagh Mawe

Grown Men - Avon Books

<u>Definition of a Dandelion - Dan'de-li'on</u>

Webster's - A well known flowered plant
of the chicory family. Abundant as a weed.

Storyteller's - Those who, coming from
limited backgrounds and with no special
attributes except imagination, courage,
and belief in themselves, rise above the
ordinary to make their lives a brilliant
example to others.

PROLOGUE

"The Spanish Armada, built high like towers and castles, rallied into the form of a crescent whose horns were at least seven miles distant, coming slowly on, and though under full sail, yet as the winds labored and the ocean sighed under the burden of it..."

William Camden
1551 - 1623

Everyone who knows the story of that doomed Armada, knows that what fearful storms began, Francis Drake, with his brilliant mind and swift ships, finished. Only a handful of the great galleons survived, mastless, riddled with shot, to limp northward off the coast of Scotland and the west coast of Ireland. Fewer still returned to Spain.

The "Black Irish" they call the descendants of those few Spaniards who, against all odds, survived to drag themselves ashore in Ireland.

The "Wild Red Devil" they called the Arabian stallion - they never having seen his like before - that appeared in their land at that same time in history.

At dawn they saw him here, at dusk there, fading in and out of the mists of that misty Isle with only the thunder of his swift receding hooves and the prints he left behind to show they had not dreamed what they saw. And he became a legend again as he had been before, in Spain. A legend in a land of legends.

He was a creature of unbelievable beauty this horse, the gift of a tribesman to a Sultan to a King.

On the day the Armada set sail from Spain, the crowds gathered to wish their ships Godspeed fell silent when, to the fanfare of trumpets, the great Arabian horse was led before them. Then, when it was learned that it was he, Almustaq, who would carry the flag bearer of Spain onto English soil and lead the invading army to victory over the Protestant queen, wild cheering broke out.

Some who saw him that day said it was the sun, turning his rich chestnut coat to flame and playing on the thick ropes of muscle flowing beneath like liquid power, that gave him his aura of unearthly brilliance.

Others said, no, it was the small perfect head with the wide-spaced eyes and the narrow muzzle that made him unique. That and his carriage. The arch of his neck. The sweep and furl of mane and tail. The elegant walk that turned to a sideways dance on legs as fine and clean and sculptured as a dancer's. As if, they said, the horse himself knew of his mission and was proud to be the chosen one.

Whatever it was, none who saw him that day ever forgot him.

Four weeks the horse was to live, imprisoned in a space scarcely larger than himself, in the stinking, airless, rat-infested hold of one of the galleons before it broke apart beneath him.

Twenty-eight terrible days they were of heaving seas and total darkness and roaring cannons and shouting, dying men. Days of sickness and hunger and thirst and pain. Days of fear and outrage and humiliation. At the end of them, the common horses and mules surrounding Almustaq were dead and he, his life flickering at every breath, nearly so.

But by then he was past hearing the sounds of battle and death, was no longer terrorized by the smell of burning and smoke that seeped down to his quarters. Drifting in and out of consciousness, he thought himself free again, racing unfettered across the hot sands of his desert birthplace, glorying in his youth and the inexhaustible strength of his limbs.

So he dreamed until there came a new sound above the shriek of the wind and the shouts of the crew. A terrifying sound that wrenched him back to consciousness, the hair of his hide on end with fear. A rumbling, moaning roar it was that grew in momentum, even as he listened, until it became a scream, and then the ship beneath him shuddered and broke apart, the seas moved in, and the scream was silenced.

Like a wild thing Almustaq fought that new terror: the thundering torrent of frigid water that engulfed him, filling his eyes and mouth and nostrils with its stinging salt. And yet, as he struggled, it came to him that he was buoyant, that the partitions that had imprisoned him for so long were gone. He knew, too, that the terrible pain in his eyes was not from salt alone, but from light as well. And he understood that the churning waters were not the enemy he had thought, but a friend.

A friend whose strength, if not opposed, would carry him away from the tomb he had lived in and set him free. So he stopped his fight, harbored his strength, and let himself become one with it. He let the towering cliffs of water take him as they willed, knowing they would ultimately carry him free of the jagged, splintered wood, the snarl of rope and sail, the lifeless corpses of man and beast that choked and moved with the seas around him.

His instinct was correct for in time the shriek of the wind lessened and the seas calmed themselves. With still more time, a full moon climbed the sky and he was alone on a tranquil sea.

All that night the great horse swam, knowing instinctively the direction of the land, perhaps smelling it, and when he grew tired, he rested, allowing the water to support him.

Daylight came slowly, softly, and his eyes adjusted with it and there was no more pain. The sun, appearing only at intervals throughout that day, was on its downward path before he saw the land he had known was there. It was dusk before he felt the first nudge of rock beneath his hooves and dark before he pulled himself out of the water and floundered, as awkwardly as on the day of his birth, across the jagged rocks at the water's edge.

XIV

He didn't - couldn't - go far. Only a few feet above the tide line to the base of a rise where his trembling legs splayed beneath him and groaning, he fell to his side. Blackness, as black as the hold of the doomed ship, overcame him and he was still for the first time since his hellish journey began.

Hunger woke him. A hunger fiercer than any he had ever known. Stiff, weak, on hooves nearly destroyed by weeks of standing in his own waste, he staggered up the small incline he had slept beside and found a mist-shrouded, green land before him. The short, wet grass there was sweet to his taste, but he was too weak to eat more than a few mouthfuls before his legs buckled and he slept again.

Many weeks he lived in this manner: sleeping and eating, eating and sleeping. Slowly his body healed and his strength returned. As more time still passed, he left the coast and wandered inland, following only his instincts and his whims. And as he grew stronger he discovered anew the exhilaration of his limbs moving fast and sure beneath him, felt again the sting in his eyes and the wind at his head that came with his own speed, and he gloried in his freedom.

He was too fast, too intelligent, too wary of a trust betrayed to ever allow man near him again. He wanted no part of them and for the remaining twenty-eight years that he lived, evaded their every futile attempt to trap him.

His offspring numbered in the dozens, his descendants in the hundreds. Dandelion was one of them, but, of course, she didn't know that...

XVI

ONE

A bold and demanding creature was Dandelion, in the early days of her life. She thought the small field she lived in at the side of McCree's cottage the center of the world and herself the most important being alive.

She thought her mother a personal possession and took it hard when, a few days after her birth, McCree came at dawn and took her away to work. Dandelion screamed her anger and resentment at their retreating backs, cried her terror and abandonment, flung her small self at the gate, and not a bit of good did it do her. She saw chickens stop their scratchings in the dust to listen to her racket; heard the windows and doors of the cottage slam shut, but her mother, strange looking between the shafts of a cart, disappeared round a turn in the lane and Dandelion was alone

A long time she kept at her protests, until her body bruised and bled and her eyes and nose streamed... Until she wore herself out and slept...

Of course her mother came back. Smelling of rain and sweat and tiredness, and then it was her that carried on. From a long way off Dandelion heard her calling, the sound of her cries mingling with the rumble of her cart bouncing over rough ground, the urgent thud of her hooves and McCree's shouts telling her to whoa then... To calm herself... Did she think he'd let harm come to her foal? But the old mare didn't listen to a word of it and only hurried the more, rounding the last bend like she was young again, like she was running the Grand

National, with McCree, red in the face, running at her side, trying to get ahead of her to open the gate to the foal before she crashed through it, cart and all.

In her ignorance Dandelion thought she had her mother back to herself again, thought the whole terrible episode a mistake on the part of McCree, who didn't know any better, and she was happy again.

The errors in her thinking became apparent the next dawn when McCree came back and took her mother away again, and the next dawn after that, too, and every dawn thereafter, except Sundays when she was given the rest she'd earned. It took Dandelion that long to understand that her mother didn't belong to her at all. Her mother belonged to McCree.

They'd been together a long time, the two of them. Twenty-eight years since he'd walked the sixty-odd miles to the Dublin Horse Fair, five years of savings in his pocket, to look for the horse he'd carried in his head ever since he could remember. He'd spotted her at once. But he was a suspicious man, McCree, and terrified of being taken for a fool, so he'd feigned indifference and taken himself off to look at others, not thinking it right a man should go to THE DUBLIN HORSE FAIR and buy the first horse he set eyes upon. But he'd watched her out of the corners of his eyes even while going through the motions of examining others and then, afraid that others might see in her what he did, hurried back and paid out his money.

The horse was a Clydesdale, and she didn't come cheap. McCree put his money on her clean legs and cool feet, her great height, the breadth of her chest and the power in her hind quarters. He also put it on the lively intelligence shining in her eyes, her long confident stride, and the feeling that she was his horse.

So they set off then, a young man and a young horse, going to make of his rock-strewn acres a profitable farm. And because the hedgerows they passed between were white with daisies, and the star on his horse's forehead looked like one too, he called her Daisy.

Heads together, like a courting couple on a Sunday afternoon, they covered the distance back to his farm in deep conversation, though never a sound passed between them. By the time they arrived, Daisy knew the whole of McCree's life and his dreams as well. She knew, without ever laying eyes on them, the lay of his lands, the rocks and trees that were to be cleared, the walls that were to be built. She knew she would plow his fields and bring in his harvests and when she was done with that, then she would do the same for their high and mighty neighbor, Lord Harrington - who owned the racing stables - and thereby earn McCree good money besides.

Every third year she was to be mated, and her foals - from such a superior mare - would fetch a fine price. It was Daisy's job then to make McCree a prosperous man. And this she did.

Over the years she threw her might and willing heart into every task set her so that, seeing her at it, people joked and said it looked as though she planned to inherit the place herself some day, such was her pride in her work. Neighboring farmers, seeing this great capacity for labor and her even disposition, put in bids for her foals before ever they were born.

Like the good soul she was, Daisy worked as well in summer's heat as winter's cold. She never fell sick, never went lame and never, in all her years of giving, asked anything for herself except the peace and freedom of her field at the end of a day.

All of the plans then, the dreams shared on the road from Dublin, came to be fulfilled with one exception: in her thirtieth year Daisy was to give birth to her last foal and that one, unlike the others, would not be sold off, but kept, a proud heir to the kingdom they had created.

McCree turned deaf ears to every offer coming his way when that time came and

Daisy's condition became apparent. "This one's for me," he told them all. "The best is always last and it's keeping it for meself I am."

He was more excited at the prospect of that final birth than at any of its predecessors (or even his own dozen children), and he lavished Daisy with every care and attention. Still, he worked her to the end, knowing the birth would go easier for her if he did.

It was plowing they worked at the day of the birth, both of them taking pride in the arrow-straight furrows furling up from the plow's blade to fill the damp air around them with the good clean smell of fresh turned earth. The smell that meant spring to both of them.

McCree was worried, yet trusting Daisy to tell him when her time came. "What about it then, me darling?" he asked each time they came to the end of the field beside the low stone farm buildings. "Will ye be after doing another there and back?"

And time after time, Daisy's reply was

to turn the mud-weighted plow back into the field and the stinging, wind-driven rain that bruised her eyes until they swelled like over-ripe plums. "It's spring, isn't it?" she'd be saying by her actions. "And who to plow if not meself?"

It was mid-afternoon then before she turned away from her work and stood waiting for the plow to be unhitched and her harness removed.

She was preoccupied then, intent on herself like a person with an appointment to keep, wanting only her own field and the privacy of the old, low-hanging trees there. The trees that had sheltered and watched over all her births.

McCree left her then, put on a show of seeing to other matters, knowing better than to attend her. But a hundred times and more he walked between cottage and barn pretending indifference to what went on beneath the trees, though worried half sick just the same. In between times he shouted at his wife and clouted any child foolish enough to get in his way. And when supper time came he pushed his plate aside unfinished, though as a rule he liked his food, McCree.

Daisy had taught him to stay away with the birth of her first. He'd hovered then, him and the young veterinarian he'd brought up from the village to protect his investment, and she'd cramped the foal in the whole of a night, not wanting him there, begging with her wheeling and fretting to be left alone to see to matters in her own way.

It was late in the night then and raining hard before McCree guessed enough time had passed for the youngster to have been born. From a long way off Daisy and her foal heard his footsteps approach. Purposeful, defiant almost, they sounded at first. Diffident, squelching on tiptoe across the wet soggy earth, they sounded as they drew close.

Slowly, murmuring endearments that only Daisy understood, McCree approached, a lantern held high over his head. He saw to the mare first, feeding her the mash he'd brought with him, assuring himself all was well before turning eagerly to the foal.

"And what have you brought me this time, me darling?" he called back to Daisy, kneeling at the side of the foal. "A pale one it is to be sure! Not your own grand coloring at all, me darling, nor that of its sire neither."

His confident chatter died away as the foal struggled to its feet. "Small it is," he muttered. "The smallest of the lot. Too small for me purposes I'm thinking... And a filly besides... And your last a grand big colt. The biggest in the county now..."

He fell silent altogether as he studied the foal's face, and it was a long time before he said at the end of a groan, "Mother of God, will you be looking at the eyes on it! Further apart than any I've ever seen and bulging besides. And the muzzle on it! Narrow as a hound's and yet the nostrils big as trumpets! Sure and it's a face to frighten the devil himself!"

Sick and black with disappointment he

was, the culmination of his grand plan shattered by the appearance of the foal. Wearily he set it aside and went to Daisy's head. "You did your best, me darling," he consoled. "Sure and 'twas the greed in me that did us in. I should of let it be three years ago and kept the last fine fellow you gave me. Well... There's nothing to be done about it now. It's a runt we're after dealing with and we'll have to make the best of it, though how it's to be done I'm not knowing."

He picked up his lantern and turned away still muttering. "A poor pale runt of a thing it is and none to blame but meself. Not fit for me carts nor me plow nor anything else. Not worth a tinker's curse!" In his despair he kicked at a clump of wild flowers. "If the truth be told, it's no more use to me than these blamed dandelions and it's meself as says so!"

TWO

A fine how-do-you-do for a new born to be kicked in the teeth as it were, and called useless...! A weed! A dandelion !

And who was he to talk, strange looking thing that he was? Well, his words might have hurt Daisy, but they meant nothing to Dandelion. She didn't know what a dandelion was that first day of her life nor anything else for that matter, all the world being new to her then. She didn't know either that she was born already a possession. She thought herself free, belonging to herself, and that is how she lived.

A busy time she had of it, too, once she saw her tantrums did nothing to keep her mother at her side and having all her own learning to do.

There was her field to discover and know, once she gave up her fruitless vigil at its gate and let her curiosity run free. It became a part of her that field. A friend, offering various shelters from the cold winds and driving rains, and a special place to stand in the mornings to catch the first warming rays of the sun. In the night, strange new things pushed up from its floor and Dandelion's mornings were kept busy nibbling and tasting all of them.

It had a stream at one end. A narrow, shallow affair with a world of life in its waters once she learned to keep herself still long enough to watch it. And a long time she puzzled at the pale wavery creature staring up at her from its bottom with large questioning eyes until it came to her that she stared at herself.

Besides Dandelion and her mother, the

field sheltered and fed other creatures too. There were rabbits and foxes. And mice and birds and insects and toads. She came to know them all. She knew where they lived and what they ate and where they went to find their food, their daily comings and goings being as familiar to her as her own.

And as all about her was different every day and yet the same, so Dandelion, too, changed and grew but was still herself. She saw it in the stream and felt it in her bones. A wisp of mane and forelock began to sprout along the crest of her neck, the fuzz that was her tail lengthened, and flesh and muscle began to thicken under her hide.

She grew in her abilities, too. From a creature that scarcely knew where it began or ended and had the devil's own time getting its feet under itself - all together and all going the same way at the same time - she became fluent. Things she could only imagine one day would come easily to her the next, though she failed to notice then, and for many a long year afterwards, how

her actions always followed her thoughts.
However that may be, her ungainly
scrambling efforts at motion soon became a
smooth trot and then she taught herself to
canter and before she knew it she had
mastered the gallop.

Dandelion was enchanted at the way her
world changed when she saw it at speed. All
the things she had known as whole, defined
and stationary, could be changed to a blur
of unfamiliar blues and greens and browns -
the earth merging with the sky and the other
way around - by the simple fact of her own
amazing speed. A speed that was checked
only by the great stone walls built by her
mother and McCree long, long ago.

Of all the things about her then, the thing
she gloried in and loved the best was
working with herself. She forgot her
loneliness and sorrow, forgot her mother
even, in the hours Daisy was away at her
work.

Every day and more each day, she whirled
and played about her small green world, wild

and dizzy with the joy of herself and what she could do. She taught herself to weave in and out of trees at a gallop, charmed at the important thud of her small hooves on the sod. She raced her own shadow and, learning from the toads, leaped the stream in a bound, enchanted to see her friends, the rabbits, flying for their lives at her swift approach.

She learned to kick up her hind legs and to stand on them too. And she learned to use her voice. Being born with it shrill, she taught herself to lower it, wanting to sound like her mother.

There being nothing in the world she liked better than showing off her accomplishments, she'd be hard at it when McCree brought her mother home in the evening.

"Am I not the swiftest creature you ever saw?" she'd be asking by her actions as she sped by. "Faster than the rabbits and the squirrels. Faster even than birds that fly!"

McCree would shake his head in disgust at her antics and trudge off to his cottage, muttering as he went, but her mother tried to be kind.

"Indeed and you are," Daisy nodded when she was through with rolling away the feel of her harness in the flat brown dirt by the gate and had drunk sparingly from the stream, taking care, in her fastidious way, not to muddy its waters with her hooves. "And if that was what you were born to do, a fine thing it would be, but running and playing is not what life is about as you will learn."

"Then what is life about?" Dandelion called, pulling up from a full gallop to walk in a curious, stiff-legged manner she'd taught herself that very day.

Her mother sniffed and when she spoke it was as if McCree spoke for her. "Work is what life is about. Work and serving your master. Clearing the land and planting the seeds. That is why you were born."

"You mean as you do?"

"Exactly."

"But I can't. I'll not be having the time.

It's meself I have to work with, there being so much I still have to learn. As I grow I will jump the walls of this small field and travel, faster than the wind, across the larger ones I see about us. I have too much to do to stop and work for another."

Her mother sighed. "Dandelion! Dandelion! Is it feathers you carry in your head in place of brains? Not even the wildest and boldest of your brothers ever talked of jumping walls and galloping off to nowhere. Why, where would you belong? Who would you work for? A horse without a master is... Well, it is nothing."

"I'll not be needing any master," Dandelion called, executing a fast little sideways step.

Her mother was deeply shocked and snorted her disapproval. "Not be needing a master? May the saints preserve us from your ideas. Tell me, is it wild horses you see running about the place with no master telling them where to go or what to do next? The very idea of such a thing!"

Dandelion galloped to the far end of the field bringing herself up short at the wall, then wheeled about on her hind legs and careened back to her mother, stopping in a skid that took her forefeet under Daisy's belly.

"And the mice and the rabbits?" she panted. "And the birds and the toads? Is McCree their master too? I don't see them running off to work the live long day as you do."

Her mother's lip curled. "It's speaking of different things, you are," she sniffed. "They are wild animals. We are tame. Since time began we horses have worked for man. We are beasts of burden. That is our destiny."

"But why...?"

"That'll be enough of your whys, Dandelion!" Her mother said sharply. "It's wearing me out with them you are. And you'll please me by not chasing about the place as though you had wasps at your tail. At least when the Master is about. It's a worry to him and meself besides. It's enough that you're small and look strange, without him thinking you're soft in the head as well. A hard-working man he is and a good master too, and it's an obliging, hard-working horse he's needing to help him through his days."

Dandelion was blessed to be away from the opinions and disapproval of the two of them enough in those early days that her high spirits and joy in herself were not dampened. Alone, she filled the green-gold days of her first summer with achievements that came to serve her well later in life.

Her first autumn drifted in with soft rains and falling leaves and a cooling sun. She saw her friends the squirrels become enemies, one with the other, fighting and jabbering over nuts, saw the birds that had lived over her head since her birth fly away, saw the toads and frogs and insects disappear. She saw her own baby coat thicken and she saw her mother worked half to death bringing in the harvests for miles around.

"And what is it then," Dandelion asked

Daisy one evening when she came home from work, "this thing called winter that has every living thing in such a state?"

But her mother, the poor soul, never answered, though Dandelion asked a dozen times. Daisy was asleep on her feet before the gate swung shut behind her.

So Dandelion learned of winter too, alone, and she gloried in it. She was exhilarated with the cold air at her head and the hardening ground at her feet making the sound of her flying hooves more impressive than ever. To be sure there was nothing left alive in her field to nibble on, but McCree threw her an armful of hay in the morning and when the weather turned colder than that, he brought the two of them into the barn at night. There they thought it grand to drowse on a warm bed of straw away from the cold earth and rain-filled, howling winds.

And so Dandelion had a taste of all the seasons, and by the time she was a year old, she knew her little world inside out and thought there was no other. She forgot what it was to be new and unsure. She thought she had lived forever and knew everything there was to know.

A rude awakening she was in for to be sure. A lifetime of learning lay ahead of her and Dandelion with ideas as narrow as her small field.

THREE

It happened that, with McCree and Daisy working as hard about their neighbor, Lord Harrington's land, as they did their own, a bargain had been struck between the two men: in exchange for Daisy's labor, Lord Harrington allowed her foals to graze with his own yearling stock until they were old enough to be broken to harness, grazing being in short supply on McCree's cultivated acres.

On a fine spring morning then, all unknowing, Dandelion stepped out of one world and into another, and the narrowness of her thinking quickly became apparent.

Fresh-groomed she was and in a dither because of it, it being her first and her not understanding the reason for it. In a dither too was McCree, vexed at her sidling and nervousness, and grudging the time she kept him from his work. If he'd had more time and the interest besides, he'd have noticed, with the mud and Dandelion's winter coat coming off under his brushes, how her once pale coloring was darkening to a rich chestnut and that she was well muscled for her age. If he'd taken the trouble to measure her with the palms of his hands from the ground to the top of her shoulders, he'd have seen she was already approaching thirteen hands and not so small after all. But next to her mother, towering at sixteen hands and wide enough to make three Dandelions, he saw her as a runt still and treated her like a fool.

He put a halter on her head and oil on her hooves and then, Daisy and her cart on one side of him, Dandelion on the other, led them out of the yard and into the lane.

Dandelion was agog, her already prominent eyes bursting out of her head in her eagerness to see for herself where it was her mother disappeared to every morning of her life.

A beautiful place she thought that leafy lane, though her pleasure in it did nothing to calm McCree's already outraged patience.

"Will you be calming yourself!" he roared as Dandelion dashed ahead the length of her rope, trying to see around each corner before they came to it.

And, "Will you be moving yourself!" as she stood transfixed at the wonder of a large lake shimmering in the sunlight.

He cursed her soundly when she went up on her hind legs at the unexpectedness of a rabbit crossing their path and begged the saints for mercy when, her attention elsewhere, she stumbled into a puddle and muddied the three of them.

"Where are we going?" she asked her mother, but too excited, too entranced by the scenes unfolding around her to listen to her reply.

Presently they turned into a long driveway and Dandelion had under her hooves the delightful, unaccustomed sound of scrunching gravel. A long time they followed the curves of that drive, in and out of parklands and through woods, and with each step Dandelion felt tension mounting within her. Her hide prickled and she broke a sweat, sensing already, picking out of the air, unfamiliar sounds and odors. A feel of excitement. Of anticipation...

One last turn they rounded and the drive opened into a large yard surrounded on all its sides by stables. Dandelion stopped so sharp she'd have had McCree on the ground if her mother hadn't been there for him to cling to.

Over the top of each stable's half door, curious horses' heads peered out. There were friendly ones among them, calling out to them, nuckering a welcome. There were jealous ones too, their ears back, not liking the interest the newcomers created. And there were the restless, turning away to prowl the straw of their stable and then, fearful of missing something, darting back to the door for another look. And ones, too, that were bored and set to yawning by the homeliness of the visitors.

Horses everywhere then! Calling shrilly, stamping iron-shod hooves on cobblestones and kicking at doors, insisting on their feed, demanding attention. And not just in stables either, but those with riders on their backs, going away somewhere, heads high, tails streaming. Anxious! Keen! And others coming back from somewhere, wet with sweat, necks drooping, exhausted.

In a turn of her head then, Dandelion saw more horses and more men than she had known existed, and she was amazed. For there were stable lads too, and jockeys and grooms. All of them calling out, whistling, jostling animals aside to get in and out of stables, cursing, pushing wheelbarrows, laughing...

Twisting and turning in tight little circles, her heart knocking with excitement, her hide a-tremble under its shine, Dandelion tried to see and hear all of it at once.

But McCree would have none of it. He had his day's work ahead of him and leaving the good Daisy where she stood, dragged Dandelion away.

It was quiet and calm out behind the stables. Old mares grazed and new foals played. Seeing them, Dandelion was reminded how grown up she was by comparison and drew herself up tall, trying to give her stride some authority. After all, she was a young lady. For a moment she was. And then her ears picked up the sound of drumming hooves and she forgot her manners and whirled about, near dragging McCree's arm out of its socket in her haste.

Through pockets of mist she saw a group of horses hurtling towards her on a fenced track. Riders were stretched out along their manes clear up to their ears, and she heard them calling out, demanding more of their mounts. All of them traveling at such urgent speed she thought the devil himself at their tails. As they came alongside, Dandelion felt the sting of flying soil in her eyes and the ground beneath her tremble. Thinking them terrorized, she was herself, and with a wrench of her head, freed herself from McCree's grip and was off after them, scattering a group of men who stood in her way.

A long time she galloped such was her fright. A longer time still before it came to her that she galloped alone and she slowed her pace to look behind.

She saw a peaceful sunlit day. No ugly demon at her tail. No frightened horses. No shouting men. Only McCree, dark as a thundercloud, walking deliberately towards her.

Averting her eyes she pretended she didn't see the man at all nor yet hear his voice calling her name in honeyed tones. She may have been young and confused by the startling events of the morning, but still she was not fool enough to believe a word of the blarney he cooed in her direction. She judged her fate to be terrible indeed, from the look of him, if she let him catch up to her before she caught up with her mother.

As though preoccupied with thoughts of her own then, out on a quiet walk of her own choosing, she set off in a direction wide of his own. She heard his boots in the long grass quicken their pace, and she picked up her own. She heard him start to run and broke into a trot - not fast, mind - but enough to keep her out of his reach without showing the panic she felt inside.

A lad caught the flying end of the rope dangling from Dandelion's halter as she made what she thought to be a casual re-entry into the yard. But her mother, standing yet where McCree had left her, was not fooled for a moment.

"Dandelion, Dandelion," she sighed, her daughter's appearance telling her everything. "You ran away! How could you?"

Gone was Dandelion's fine grooming. Streaked with sweat she was, her mane awry, her hooves muddied and, at her tail, a worse demon than any she had imagined - McCree.

"And is this what caused me to lose me stop watch then?" a voice called, and a man detached himself from a group standing nearby and walked towards them.

Mcree's face turned darker yet. He was ashamed of Dandelion's antics and angry as well. Quickly he snatched his hat from his head. "Aye, me Lord, the same it is, and if you'll be telling me the price of the watch I'll pay you for it and it's sorry I am for the bother," he answered, taking Dandelion's rope from the lad and making to hurry her off.

"Not so fast," Lord Harrington called, walking towards them. "You'll not be telling me you bred this one out of Daisy, will you?"

"Aye, me Lord, the same. And it's thinking meself lucky I am that it weren't the first or there'd never have been a second."

"And what were you mating her with, eh? A Shetland pony?"

The men had a fine laugh at those words, though they meant nothing to Dandelion.

McCree scowled. " 'Twas the same sire as fathered her others, me Lord, only me old Daisy was past it and meself thinking her good still for another."

"A throwback is what you've got there," another man, a veterinarian, said. "That's Arab blood you're seeing in that head."

"Arab blood?" McCree fairly spat. "Why, that's foreign blood! No wonder it's spending its days racing about like it's got feathers in its head in place of brains. Flighty it is and vain besides, and not a soul in the county willing to buy her off me. It's getting me money back I should be doing if it's Arab blood I'm having to deal with."

"She'll be settling down in a year or so," the veterinarian said. "Might make you a nice saddle horse in time."

"Saddle horse?" McCree screamed with even more indignation than he had shown at the mention of Arab blood. "And what in blazes would I be wanting with a saddle horse? It's a work horse I'm needing, and if you'll excuse me now sirs, it's to me work I'll be going. Where will you be wanting me to put it?"

"You'll find the yearlings in the south meadow same as always," Lord Harrington answered turning away.

"There's a year yet before she'll be good for anything," the veterinarian called after them. "A lot can happen in a year..."

McCree made no answer, but, his fist tight on the halter under Dandelion's jaw so she could scarcely move her head, hurried her away to the south meadow.

It was a beautiful place that meadow, rolling and sweeping off to the far horizon. It was large enough for the whole of McCree's land to fit inside with space left over on all its sides. Great trees towered about its boundaries and stands of them clustered within. It was a fitting home for the fine thoroughbreds living in its lush interior. Not that Dandelion saw any of it that day, all her attention being taken by the field's occupants.

Thirty or more of them there were, all born in the same spring as Dandelion, crowding and jostling each other along the fence, vying with each other for their first view of the strangers whose coming they had sensed long before they came into view.

Many a beautiful thing Dandelion was to see in her long life, but nothing to compare with those young horses, all crowded together in their many colorings as she saw them that first morning. Not that she didn't think them strange, for she did. How could she not when all she knew of the horse before that day was her mother's stocky frame? But these thoroughbreds were tall, their height coming from long legs that looked like sticks to Dandelion after her mother's massive fetlocks. They were slender too, more like her own width, and their movements quick and sleek. Their faces were long and narrow and they held their haughty heads high, as though nothing in the world was quite as superior as themselves.

They had an easier time of it though, studying Dandelion, than the other way around, for she had McCree's heavy hand on her halter, pulling her head this way and that, trying to get her through the gate and not one of them willing to let her pass.

It was a shock at the last to find herself alone - dwarfed - in the midst of those arrogant creatures, being pushed and jostled from every side and McCree, muttering yet, walking away over the hill. He seemed dear and familiar to Dandelion then, and she was saddened to see him go, he being the last remnant of the only life she had ever known.

"Don't leave me here," she shrilled to his retreating back. "Take me back to me darling mother and me little field. I'll calm meself... Be like me mother... Better than me mother..."

But he paid her no mind. The last of his old hat disappeared behind the crest of the hill, and she was left to make the best of it.

"What a cry baby," a dappled gray with a dark muzzle sniffed.

"I'll thank you to be keeping your opinions to yourself," Dandelion said with a toss of her head.

"It's frightened she is," said a tall black, her lip curling. "I can hear the heart in her knocking from here."

"Frightened, is it?" Dandelion snorted. "And why would I be frightened by the likes of you?"

"Because you are so small and funny looking and we are thoroughbreds."

"I'm not understanding your meaning," Dandelion said.

"Why do you have such a strange looking face?" the rude gray asked.

"Yes, why?" repeated half a dozen others.

"Your eyes are too far apart."

"Yes, they are. And too big besides."

"Why are you so little? Are you a pony?"

"Your muzzle is very narrow."

"And your nostrils are very large."

Dandelion felt their criticism like

hailstones on her back, and she tossed her head so her forelock covered the confusion she knew to be showing in her eyes. She had thought her appearance to be a matter of concern only to McCree, but in the stable yard and again in the meadow she had learned otherwise. At a loss as to how to come to her own defense, Dandelion was speechless until she remembered the only kind words ever spoken of her by a human.

"I am as I am," she told them, feigning a hauteur she did not feel, "because I have Arab blood."

She couldn't have said a wiser thing if she'd thought about it the rest of her life. No more than herself did they know the meaning of "Arab blood," and so they were silenced.

Dandelion used her advantage to clear herself a path through their midst, but they were not through with her then nor yet for many a long month to come.

"Who is your mother?" one of them called after her.

"Why, me mother is Daisy," she replied, thinking the question kind.

"Daisy?" chorused thirty voices all at the one time.

"Aye. Daisy."

"What races has she won?"

"Me mother doesn't race," she told them. "She doesn't believe in speed. Me mother works for the farmer McCree."

"Works?"

"Aye. She works. She pulls a plow. And a cart..."

"She means her mother is a farm horse," one of them gasped. "How common!"

"Our mothers are race horses," the chestnut preened. "Famous race horses..."

All together then, all at one time so that none of them made a bit of sense, the thoroughbreds began bragging of their fine mothers and their champion sires. Of bloodlines and heritage. Of races they would win and records they would break.

Dandelion left them to it, backing away slowly so that her leave taking wouldn't bring down fresh insults on her tired head. She knew nothing of Derbys or Grand Nationals or the like, and she didn't take kindly to their pushy ways and arrogant manners.

She was bewildered and confused. A short walk she had taken from McCree's small farm to Lord Harrington's fine estate, and a wide world of difference lay in between. And she had gone from being the center of one to an outcast in the other, and she felt her ignorance sorely.

FOUR

Dandelion stayed off to herself all of that first day, long after her temper had been replaced by curiosity. Her sheltered life had given her no experience in making friends, especially with so boisterous a crowd, and in any case, Lord Harrington's great meadow offered her such a variety of food after the meager grasses she'd shared with her mother, she was kept busy nibbling and tasting the whole of the day.

But horses are gregarious by nature, the herd instinct in them strong still, despite thousands of years as man's servants, and so, preoccupied as she may have seemed, she moved ever closer to those exotic creatures she was to live amongst.

She came to see she was more like them than she was like her mother.

"Flighty!" Daisy would have snorted seeing them revel, unabashed at their own beauty and freedom, outrunning their shadows one moment, striking exaggerated poses the next.

And "temperamental," she would have called their fierce squabblings, their wild joy, their sulks, their jealous tantrums.

But Dandelion understood them perfectly, for not only did she share their youth, but she sensed in them what she sensed in herself: a yearning, overwhelming desire to express themselves.

Understand, of course, that animals do not measure themselves by possessions as humans do. No. An animal has only itself...

It did not take her long then to become one of them, and they, each in their own special way, became as familiar and dear to her as the small creatures that had filled her first year.

With more time still passing, Dandelion forgot her humble beginnings and the role she was born to play. She saw her mother and McCree from time to time, sometimes working in a field close by her own, other times at a distance, always a cart or plow at Daisy's back. Fervent hellos she shrilled at the start, keeping pace with them on her own side of the fence. But as she became immersed in her grand new life, her interest in them dwindled, and at the end she scarcely raised her head at their passing. They were a part of her past with no role to play in her present. For didn't she live the life of a thoroughbred now? And hadn't she become, in her own mind at any rate, a race horse? Indeed she had.

And how could she not? She was a young and impressionable soul, and fast besides. And didn't she live their life? And dream their dreams? Intentionally and unintentionally then, she adopted their mannerisms, their easy stride, and through association became as much a race horse as her mother had become a part of McCree.

To an unknowing onlooker those horses would have appeared as no more than a group of high-spirited, untamed youngsters brawling through their days while, in truth, they were creatures earnestly learning about themselves and each other through their one great passion. Speed.

In that regard, Dandelion learned that there were those with great natural talent, but a spirit too small and mean to give of it. They were spiteful beasts, jealously hoarding their precious gift for fear others might profit just from watching them. Yet, others, with only half the ability, had such great giving hearts they'd go until they dropped, trying to drag one more ounce out of themselves or in helping others.

They had their braggarts too. Loudmouths who wore them all out with their tales of what they could do and what they would do, but were never seen in the doing. Dandelion thought them silly things until she understood that it was their own fear of failing that kept them always on the sidelines, exercising their mouths instead of their limbs.

She saw fear of failing in others, too. In those who called "liar" and "cheat" at the first sign of weakness in themselves. And in those who made excuses the length of the day, wanting more sun and less wind, a better night's sleep, more and different food...

Whatever the differences in their temperaments and personalities, however, the focal point of all their lives was speed. And from sun up to sun down they strove to go faster... further... In hot sun or drenching rain, whether whipped by wind or numbed with cold, they raced. Singly and in pairs and in a great thundering herd.

And when they rested in the heat of the day under the great oaks, or at night, their thoughts and dreams were of speed and how to do more and better.

How they dreamed! Of the races they

would win... The records they would set...
The certain fame that awaited them. The very
thought of it all enough, sometimes, to send
them rocketing out into the moonlight in the
joy and expectation of it all.

Dandelion had a long way to go to catch
up with them, and at the outset, before she
forgot her beginnings, she gave herself not
a moment's peace. Never before had she had
a yardstick, so to speak, to measure herself
against, nor competition to set her on edge.
The games of her youth, played alone in her
small field, were a far cry from matching
herself against the finest blood in Ireland,
with space enough to go the distance. But
she was fierce in her determination to equal
them and so, long after the thoroughbreds
had taken themselves off to rest under the
trees, Dandelion would still be hard at work
forcing herself to lengthen her stride,
teaching herself to hold something back for
the finish, smoothing out her starts...

Not that she still didn't like her moments
of solitude. Too many months of her life had

she lived alone not to have the need of them. Besides, it was in those quiet moments, particularly when she drifted between sleep and wakefulness, that the answers to difficulties often came to her.

For example, there was the time she was teaching herself to canter figure-eights and coming to the crossover in the middle, her legs would tangle beneath her, bringing her up short time after time.

The aggravation of it sent her off to brood in a corner and there, dozing, she saw in her head, clear as the nose in front of her, how it should be done. It was a simple matter of understanding that as she crossed the center point, her circle went off in the opposite direction. The solution then was to change stride at the center point, so that her inside legs always led in the direction the circle took her.

No sooner did she see it than she was doing it, and by nightfall her flying change was flawless, just the way she'd seen it in her head.

The only thing she failed to notice again was the connection between her thoughts and her actions, but that simple little fact, that cornerstone of life, escaped her still.

Happy, happy days those were and all of them too young to know it. They were eager to have them done and over and themselves full grown and gone. Dandelion expected, not knowing her time there limited, to have one of Lord Harrington's grooms come riding over the hill, single her out, attach a halter to her head and lead her away to a grand future, for such was the fate of one after another of her companions.

It saddened her later, thinking how eagerly they had pressed towards those grooms, each of them sure in their own hearts that their time had come. For she was to learn later that while racing made men rich, it made horses old before their time, their good years over in a handful of seasons and only the best retained for breeding, while the rest were sold off to work they were not suited for, and many a tragic end besides.

But none of them knew that at the time, and they strode off into their futures, those beautiful darlings, with never a backward glance at the only happy times most of them would ever know.

They sulked, those left behind, wondering why another had been chosen over themselves, though each, at their departure, was sorely missed by those who remained. It took Dandelion a long time to realize that they were all part of a whole, each unwittingly playing a role, and when one left, all were diminished.

FIVE

They came for Dandelion on a Sunday after mass. Not Lord Harrington's groom on a fine horse but her mother and McCree.

It is true she'd forgotten them entirely, yet, seeing them crest the hill, a halter in McCree's free hand, she knew why they were there and she bolted. Finding she was not to be enticed by sweet talk, nor carrots in the palm of his outstretched hand, nor yet by Daisy's pleas, McCree left for reinforcements. He brought back two grooms with him, mounted, and the battle for Dandelion's freedom began.

Hours it was before they separated her from her conspiring friends who, with her at their center, galloped like bandits making off with a prize. Longer still before they trapped her in a corner, forced a halter over her outraged head and led her away, a prisoner, a possession again.

Terrible it was for Dandelion to find herself back in the narrow confines of a world she thought to be her past. Humiliating to have her hard-earned skills and new-found assurance snatched away by as simple an act as a gate slamming shut at the back of her. And that by a man who despised her.

Thinking her heart broken and her life destroyed, Dandelion fretted and railed and wore a path inside the towering walls of the field with her frenzied pacing. And it did her no more good than her crying had done when she was newborn and left without a mother. She felt trapped by the circumstances of her birth, and she cursed the day McCree had taken himself off to Dublin and bought her mother. With all her young heart she wanted to race, and she was going to have to pull a plow.

Often she wondered what it was in her that could not accept the life she had been born to as her mother accepted hers, with never a thought. She doubted Daisy had ever once questioned what she was or how it might have been otherwise. Nor, for all their flighty imaginings, had she ever heard a thoroughbred yearn to be other than it was.

Not that she gave up on her dreams. Not at first anyway. On the contrary, finding them thwarted, her determination to be more than a plow horse grew stronger than ever, and she thundered about the small field until the stars paled in the sky. A savage pleasure it gave her too, hearing McCree curse her noise in the middle of a summer's night. A small enough sacrifice, a night's sleep, she thought, when weighed against what he had taken from her.

Daisy had no time for her ranting. She was short with Dandelion, brushing aside her dreams and ambition as youthful folly, something she had expected her to outgrow. Dandelion saw her mother then as old. Old and set in her ways. To be sure, she had been old all Dandelion's life, but she had not known it until she met up with youth.

They had a battle royal, McCree and Dandelion, in the matter of her schooling. In her he had a rebellious, unwilling student who fought bitterly the hard metal he forced in her mouth and every one of the leather contraptions he strapped about her head and her body.

No Saint Patrick was he himself. To break a horse in such a way that the animal becomes an interested, willing partner needs love and understanding and respect. McCree had none of them, nor the pride he'd had in her mother. He took Dandelion's natural boldness as something to be crushed, whipped out of her, and in so doing he made her sullen and arrogant. And because he had her in such a state of nerves she couldn't make head nor tails of the commands he gave her, he saw her as dull and stupid as well.

It was a terribly frustrating time for both of them. A daily war with never a winner. But he was a stubborn man, McCree. Dandelion had been bred to take her mother's place, and he never thought to change his plan, small and flawed though he saw her. And if she learned nothing else in her year of schooling, she learned that he would not give up, but come back, day after day, until a victory of sorts was his.

To be sure, the victory was a compromise, for at the end of a year, with Dandelion's bold confidence stripped away and tentative uncertainty in its place, he was obliged to work her as a team with Daisy, hoping to balance the youth and strength of the one against the patience and experience of the other and so temper what he called the "foreign devil" in Dandelion.

A strange-looking pair they made, the mother and the daughter, when harnessed side by side, each making the other look larger and smaller by comparison. There was Daisy, tall and poised, her mane a-flutter of bright ribbons braided in by McCree, her walk as confident and regular as the ticking of a clock. And there was Dandelion, her harness an ill-fitting mess of patched hand-me-downs, her uncertainty showing in the whites of her eyes, the sweat on her hide, and her legs pumping two strides to Daisy's every one.

"Me Grace and me Disgrace," McCree called them, joking to hide his humiliation at the laughter they caused on market days and in their rounds about the district.

Dandelion felt disgraced too. Mortified to be seen, a wretched cart at her heels, when she knew herself capable of so much more. And never more so than when their work took them to Lord Harrington's. For then it was the heads of Dandelion's friends that showed at the half doors of each stable to call cheery greetings and their hooves that thundered past her on the practice track.

"Don't be counting me out yet!" she wanted to call out after them. "Many's the one of you I beat in me time and I'll be coming back to show you." But she never uttered a sound. Instead she turned her head the other way, pretending preoccupation in her own work as though what they did was of no interest to her.

A wise move it was, nevertheless, to work Dandelion alongside her mother, for with Daisy there, her anxieties lessened, her trembling and sweating at McCree's approach stopped and she began to understand, at last, the meaning of the various shouts, snorts, whistles and hisses that were his commands.

A certain confidence began to grow in her then, and as it did, McCree's angry shouts lessened and her mother beamed her approval. Dandelion liked to think she helped her mother too in those times, for Daisy was a very old horse indeed by the time Dandelion took her place at her side. Her eyesight was failing and sometimes her stride faltered and she stumbled. If a morning were cold or damp, Daisy's limbs would stiffen, and she'd work half a day before they moved free.

If Dandelion had known there was such a thing as death, she would have doubled her efforts and tried so much harder to be the heir she was supposed to be. She would have given Daisy peace from her everlasting complaining, and thrown all her heart into her work so that McCree, delighted, would have retired Daisy to the small field she loved and let her finish out her life in peace.

But Dandelion knew nothing of death until Daisy taught her of it with her own.

SIX

It remained a hard thing for Dandelion, all of her life, to think of her mother's death and the events leading up to it. Such ordinary goings-on they were that had they not been the final acts of a life, not one of them could have been brought to mind a day later. As it was, every second, every detail of that terrible day was blazed into her head forever.

Rain had started in the night so the dawn was late in coming, but not their master. A punctual man he was. As punctual as he was stubborn and Daisy, knowing this, roused herself each dawn to watch for a light in the cottage, that being her signal to make her way to the gate with Dandelion, an unwilling partner, whining at her side.

Misery it was that day to leave the snug shelter of wall and trees and stand about in the cold at the gate to accommodate McCree.

With the heavens pouring and the earth deep in mud, McCree passed over their grooming that morning and set them straight to their breakfast. Daisy was single-minded when it came to her feed. She wanted no interference. No idle chatter. Only privacy. And McCree obliged her in this, busying himself with other things until she turned away from her trough, ready to be sociable again.

"It's me ruin that's falling this morning," McCree called to her from the open door where he stood watching the rain gust across the yard. "The work of a summer out there drowning... Going for nought... And me horses standing idle besides..."

A dozen alternatives to his disrupted plans he voiced and rejected before fetching out their harness. "It's the old stump we'll be clearing away today, me darling," he told Daisy. "The one up on the hill yonder we was talking about the other day. A blemish to me land it is and a long time I've had a mind to pull it out."

To Dandelion the old stump was a part of the landscape, and once McCree's intentions were clear she wondered why a man would tax himself removing such a natural thing. But she knew better than to ask her mother the whys of it. She was not so young anymore as to not know there were things even Daisy could not fathom.

Wind and rain alike slapped at them as they made their way up the hill and waited in the half-light for McCree to see to his part of the work. A long, nerve-wracking time it took him too, chopping away at the roots with his ax. A time in which both horses grew cold, and Dandelion began to fidget as though perhaps she sensed what was to come.

However that may be, McCree was

satisfied at the last and backed Dandelion into place, positioning her so that she faced downhill. With only a nod from him, Daisy backed her own self into place in front of Dandelion and waited while McCree attached long chains to both their collars.

He stood a way off from them then and, raising his arm, waited for their ears to be listening, particularly Dandelion's, and when he was sure they were, brought his arm down sharp, gave a shout, and the horses threw their weight forward into their collars. Dandelion heard the chains snap tight and in front of her, saw her mother's massive haunches strain and her great hooves chew the earth. Sweat broke on both of them and they felt their eyes bulge and sting at their efforts.

There came another shout and Daisy, understanding it, stopped her pulling while McCree strode back to determine their progress.

"Devil an inch the brute's given," he called and reaching for his ax, set to chopping again.

The blade made a dull thudding sound as it bit into sodden wood and earth, and at each thud Dandelion shivered, fearing the ten feet of tree still standing would come crashing down on her back.

Daisy, her patience as long as the day, had no such foolish notions in her head and stood as she always did, head drooping, one hind leg resting, sweat and rain dripping off every side of her. She straightened up sharp enough though at the sound of McCree squelching back through the mud to her head.

Again he raised his arm and Dandelion readied herself, throwing her weight forward at his command at the same time as her mother.

Again and again, as the rain worsened and the ground beneath their hooves churned into a slippery mire in which they fought for a foothold, they pulled and stopped, pulled and stopped.

McCree's determination to see the job

through grew with each failed attempt and yet, at each new effort, they were brought up short. He thought to loosen the roots by working the horses sideways. A few measured paces to the left, the command to pull, then a few to the right...

Around them the air grew thick with the smell of deep earth uncovered and decaying wood and the sweat that lathered and guttered off both horses.

As the day wore on, Dandelion felt the tension in her growing so that, even in times of waiting, she could not be still. She shook where before she had trembled. She tried, foolish as it was, to free herself, going up on her hind legs until McCree's whip brought her down sharp. But she'd reached the limits of her patience and was no longer capable of the concentration he demanded. She was numbed by the everlasting shouts to pull and to whoa. The cries for more of this and less of the other. She was sick of the mud sucking at her hooves. The chafe of harness rubbing through to her flesh, the thirst in her throat, the sweat stinging her eyes. Most of all she was sick of that ancient tree clinging as firmly to its hill as McCree clung to its removal.

Oh, he had his way in the end. Over the roar of the wind, the grinding of the chains, their own blood pounding in their ears, they heard his shout of triumph, felt the immovable begin to move.

He was at their heads then, directing them to pull at angles, first this way, then the other. Inches at a time they fought that stump out of its centuries-old bed.

And still he asked for more, calling for their dregs. And as he asked, they gave. Time after time until abruptly, Daisy was done with her giving. She was dead. Dead as she had lived, on her feet.

Dandelion was a stranger to death, but seeing her mother slowly sinking before her, she knew Daisy would never get up again.

So it was her mother Dandelion pulled off the hill that day then, her heart as heavy as Daisy's weight, with McCree stumbling and sobbing at her side, and the stump, its exposed roots pointing   skywards, that remained. A fitting monument to the stubbornness of a man like McCree.

SEVEN

At her mother's death Dandelion understood what she had begun to suspect while she lived: that Daisy's life, as humble and simple as it had always seemed to her, was as spectacular in its own way as any of Lord Harrington's fine champions. A simple soul she had thought her and dull as well until she took her place beside her. Then Daisy's skill and knowledge, her way of making difficult tasks appear easy, earned her love and respect. Daisy had given dignity and class to everything she had touched. And with her grand majestic presence gone from the place, everything seemed smaller and shabbier, and McCree a lesser man.

A lost soul he was without her, as though Daisy striding at his side had given him his identity and without her he forgot who he was. She had been the best part of his life and when she died, his ambition died with her. Certainly he grieved more for Daisy than the two sons killed in the Great War. More, doubtless, than he would have for his shrewish wife, had he outlived her. For Daisy had never argued with him to waken the dead nor made demands of him, nor called him an old fool gone soft in the head, words often hurled at his back as he left of a morning.

Dandelion grieved for her mother too, and saw herself, too late, as Daisy had done: excitable and nervous one moment, petulant and uncooperative the next. Too late she tried to be like her, hoping Daisy would somehow know that her last offspring, though small, had a heart as big as her own and the willingness, at last, to fill the role she was born to play.

Filled with good intentions she was and determined to win the respect of McCree with her hard work and willingness, as Daisy had done. Gladly she threw herself and all of her heart into her work only to be brought up, time after time, by his harsh words and the sting of his whip. And each night she was returned to her field, her ears ringing with his curses where her mother's had rung with his praise.

It took her a long time to understand she could no more be her mother, so different were their temperaments, than she could turn herself into a cabbage. A double burden she put on herself then with her efforts at patience and interest and willingness - all foreign to her - together with the heavy burden of her work. One life we have to live, as ourselves, and not as poor imitations of others.

Little by little then, a day at a time, Dandelion's high ideals left her. The self-confidence she had begun to feel at her mother's side wore away under McCree's unkind criticism and comparisons. She became tentative again, unsure of herself, and then, because she had no liking or interest in her work, bored and frustrated. She turned surly and defiant for a while and then she stopped feeling at all. She gave up on herself.

She was exhausted - numb - not knowing that when a mind is not taken with its work, no matter that it consume all of its time, a boredom and irritability sets in more exhausting than any labor devised.

A sorry, sorry pair they became, McCree and Dandelion. Not a shred of trust or affection was there between them, and each taking the other for a fool besides. Not for him would Dandelion bestir herself of a morning to watch for his light but made him wait, knowing that his hand on her halter would be rough and unkind, her food meager, and her work hard and thankless. Nor did he bother with grooming her or cleaning her harness or stringing leaves and flowers about her bridle to help with the flies as he had done for her mother.

And so they dragged through their days, each lost in their own bitter thoughts, each blaming the other for the miserable entrapment of their existence, yet neither knowing how, nor having the energy, to make a change.

At times it gave Dandelion a certain pleasure to act clumsy and stupid when she saw her actions added to McCree's difficulties. And she was not above taking her cart through a gate too sharp so that it clipped the post or better yet, got stuck.

And McCree, too, could look the other way and pretend ignorance if Dandelion's harness started to rub her sore or if there were mice droppings scattered throughout her food.

Well, had Dandelion known then, as she did later, that it is expectations that make a day or a life, and not circumstances or what others say or think, she'd have changed her attitude very quickly. But she was not so wise, and her days therefore, were no more nor less than what she expected with no end in view to their dreary repetition until, quite by chance, or so it seemed, she set herself free.

EIGHT

Not that Dandelion's running away can be seen as the act of a rebel though doubtless her story would have more "dash" if she had been so bold. But by then she had become far too much of a mindless drone to plan or execute so daring - not to say wicked - a deed. And if the truth is to be told, Dandelion didn't even run. Rather, she walked, amazing herself at every step, and with many a backward glance.

Her vanishing, as it were, took place on

a summer's night. It was an unusually hot night and insects were plaguing the life out of her. Half-crazed by their bites and stings she was and she rolled herself more than once in the flat, worn earth by the side of the gate. When that failed to stop her itching, she rubbed herself up against the gate itself, and as she did so, she heard a sharp cracking sound that frightened her half out of her wits and sent her flying across her field in a panic. A long while she waited before venturing back to determine the cause of the noise.

She was astonished to see the old iron latch pulled free of its rusted nails and the post securing the gate tilted sideways. Still, she had no thought of leaving and it was only a vapid curiosity that made her nudge that teetering post with her nose. There was a soft thump, and a puff of dust, and the old post lay on its side, half buried in weeds and nettles that quivered at its impact. The gate swung free.

It must have been instinct that carried her forward since the part of her brain given to thinking and making decisions was in such a sorry state of disuse. It was as though a sharp voice commanded, "Go!" and, without a moment's hesitation, she went.

All night she obeyed that other part of herself. Unerringly, it took her off the path where her hooves might have been heard and into the thicker grass bordering its sides, while her usual, everyday self looked back over its shoulder, askance, dismayed, wondering at what was happening.

Not hurrying, but not dawdling either, she skirted the farm yard and, still without a thought she could call her own, yet without a moment's hesitation, turned away from the paths that made up her daily rounds. Nothing stopped or hindered her. She pushed through hedges, jumped walls and waded streams.

As the night wore on, the shock of what she was doing lessened and her thinking processes started up again. She wondered, as she advanced through the moonlight, if there were a part of her that never slept but had waited, biding its time, for the chance to set her on a path of her own.

In no time at all she was in country unfamiliar to her for, in all her life, she had never traveled more than a few miles in any direction from her birth place. The land she now covered was hillier and wilder than any she had trod before.

For a long time she puzzled over the ease with which she traveled until it came to her that she was without her wretched cart and all the trappings that went with it. That long it took her to realize she was free! No longer a beast of burden! Free to do as she pleased for the rest of her life! The thought of it brought her up short to shake her head and then the rest of herself in amazement.

With the shackles of her previous master gone from her body, the fatigue she associated with them was gone too. Likewise, the frustration and boredom that had made of her a poor dumb beast of burden.

Pride in what she had unwittingly done infused her like a tonic. Her head, that had not been higher than her withers in years, came up sharp, and she arched her neck to hold it firm. Making a banner of her tail, she turned herself sideways to the path a little and broke into a canter. Then seeing ahead of her an open stretch of land, she barreled into it, half mad with the joy of herself and the freedom to do as she pleased.

Not one of her paces had she forgotten. As fast as she remembered one, another came to mind. She went from tight circles to ever-widening ones, and then she remembered her figure eights and the flying change, and she performed them all as though there had been no intervening, wasted years.

There were no walls where she played in the moonlight and yet, because she excelled at stopping from full gallop to pivot, and because since her earliest days she had been forced to develop the muscular control it required - a control none of her thoroughbred friends had ever equaled - she did that too. Time after time she brought herself up short and whirled off in another direction just for the fun of it.

The breath was gone from her before she remembered she was running away and took herself back to the path she followed.

She was hungry and tired too but dawn had come. Doubtless, she thought, McCree even then was staring in shocked disbelief at the sight of the open gate and the empty field. She wondered how long he'd search for her before asking for Lord Harrington's lads and horses and dogs to help him.

She took to her heels at the thought, but not as a fool. She had sense enough not to cross open fields or walk along the crest of hills, but stayed close to hedgerows and walls and plunged through thickets and woods that otherwise she might have skirted.

As the days passed, however, with never a sight nor sound of pursuers, her sense of urgency let up and she gave herself the pleasure of fine grazing and good shelter when she came upon them, though she was not so careless as to tarry long in any one place.

Not that she saw no humans as she traveled. She did. They were everywhere for her to see as she skirted cottages and farms and small villages. But the fact was she developed a sixth sense, as it were, and always knew if they were about well before they knew of her, and not once, in all the time of her freedom, did she ever come face to face with any of them.

There were horses for her to see, too, as she traveled. Some she saw working in the way she had worked herself and others in ways she had not known existed. Contented creatures they were for the most part, going through their days as her mother had done, with never a question. But she also saw cruelty. Abuse that saddened her and made her think that McCree, for all his stubborn, stupid ways, had been a mild master by comparison.

She saw good willing beasts pulling loads that were far too heavy for them, loads that would have made a team falter, and whipped for their trouble. And she saw beasts so thin and underfed the wonder was they walked at all. And others being teased and tormented by ignorant children, their hands full of rocks and sticks and their mouths with ugly words.

She saw horses penned in filthy yards with no grazing nor water. And horses tied up so short they could not move their heads to clear out the flies that gorged in the corners of their eyes.

Seeing those poor tormented beasts was enough to make her heart ache, and yet, her new-found freedom gave her a certain arrogance and, forgetting that she had not had the wits to plan her own escape, she wondered why they did not leave as she had done. Well... she had no way of knowing then that her joy in her own freedom was soon to come to an end.

NINE

Huntsmen it was that were the start of Dandelion's troubles.

She first heard the call of a huntsman's horn on a glorious autumn morning. The air about her was quick and clear from a night frost, and the sound carried from far, far away. A strange, unfamiliar cry it was, sounding like nothing she'd ever heard before.

Curious, yet cautious, she made her way upwards through the woods in which she found herself. It was a long climb, higher and further than she would have gone for her own pleasure, but she was uneasy and would not rest until she discovered the source of that mournful, unknown sound.

Again and again as she climbed she heard the long sorrowful wail, and then her ears picked up another sound which, listening closely, she determined to be the baying of hounds. Many, many hounds.

Panting from her exertions and more than a little uneasy, she came at last to a clearing at the top, and peering out saw, breaking from a covert far below, a fox in full flight. In no time at all the first of the hounds appeared at the back of him and in the blink of an eye the whole of her view was filled with the pack, their throats bursting with noise, and at their heels, horses and riders.

Fear made her hide prickle. Fear for herself and fear for the fox that ran, a fool could see, for his very life.

All morning from her hidden viewpoint, Dandelion followed the chase with terrible fascination, and as she watched, her admiration and respect for the fox grew. The cunning of the fellow as he led the whole hysterical pack across an open field only to double back and appear, to her view, behind them! Time after time he threw them off his scent and left them in lost, bewildered confusion while he made off in another direction.

They caught him in the end though, poor fellow. It saddened her to see so much courage and wit destroyed by the frenzied hounds. And it terrified her to think what they'd do to her if ever they found her. And that was not to be the end of it, as she thought at the death. It was just the beginning. For there were other foxes and other hunts, and it seemed to Dandelion that they were out to catch every fox in Ireland.

In every kind of weather, no matter how much distance she might put between herself and a pack in the dark of night, there were always others the next day and the sound of their horns came to haunt her dreams. Their persistence forced her to keep to the highest hills out of their way and she became, in her own mind, at least, as hunted as any fox.

Gone were the idle days of grazing freely and playing in the sun. There was little food for her on the rocky high ground and less shelter. The days shortened, the winds blew colder and, a day at a time, Dandelion's grand sense of adventure left her.

When the ground froze and the snows came, her hunger forced her, at dead of night, to the low grounds and even to small isolated farms where she searched the hedgerows and farmyards for stray wisps of hay pulled from a passing wagon at harvest time or fallen from a farmer's pitchfork between stable and barn.

Now when she considered her own pitiful state, she was reminded of the scorn she had felt for the horses she had thought abused and neglected. A mouthful of food a day, even from the hand of a cruel master, was surely better than no food at all. She envied all such animals and wild ones too, for didn't they have their own stores of food and warm burrows besides?

Her misery eventually became so great that once or twice she even thought of returning to McCree. With hindsight, her life there seemed charmed with him serving her food twice a day and bringing her in to sleep on a warm bed of straw when the nights grew cold. She had enjoyed a better life by far than the one she was presently leading, alone and starving on a bitter hilltop, with no companion or master to care if she lived or died and her hooves broken and bleeding from digging through ice and snow in search of a pitiful blade of grass. And what a fuss and bother she had made of pulling her small cart and her little plow now and then! She had been privileged and too stupid to know it.

The buoyancy that had carried her giddily forward all summer was gone. She became as tentative and unsure as she had been with McCree, but now she had only herself to blame. Each fork in the road left her hesitating. To go this way or that? To go forward in search of food or back to certain shelter?

The folly of what she had done filled her waking hours and her dreams besides. Self-pity gnawed at her as ferociously as hunger. She grew afraid, and in letting in one fear, others, like leaves before the wind, followed.

She didn't know where she was going or why. She had no purpose and no destination. She thought herself hunted and knew herself starved. She had thought herself free and yet she found no place to stop and make a life for herself. She was no freer than at the time of her birth or in the thick of her worst days with McCree. And worse than all of it was her loneliness.

It was a terrible thing, she found, to have no living creature to greet each morning. To have no mother. No friend. No small animals. No insect even with whom to pass the time of day. It seemed that nothing lived or moved in those frozen hills save herself. A hearty welcome she would have given to flies, to wasps, to the devil himself if a moment of his companionship could save her from the terrible, wrenching monotony of her own despairing thoughts.

Dandelion was lost. As lost within herself as she was in the cold winter landscape. And how was it, she wondered, that she was what she was, alive on the earth and yet belonging nowhere, with no part to play? Then it was she heard her mother's voice in the past saying, "I was born to work." And the race horses saying, "We were born to race..." Each sure and certain of their place and the meaning of their lives.

Was she destined to roam her life away, fearing man and cut off from her own kind? Was there no contribution she could make with her hard-won abilities? Was she to be useless and outcast all her life? She didn't know. She didn't know...

Some days she hurried forward, panic driving her on, searching the sky, sniffing the wind, looking for food, for shelter, for a place to belong. Other days, she was overcome with such black despair she couldn't move, but dozed a fitful sleep that exhausted her, with dreams as barren and frightening as the winter sky.

At the last she was too light-headed to know what she was doing... couldn't remember where she was going. And then, on a moonless night, stumbling blindly through a snowstorm, she lost her footing and fell. Dazedly and repeatedly she tried to raise herself, but the ice was too slick. Exhaustion finally stilled her and remembering she didn't know where to go if she were upright, she stayed where she had fallen.

Once again, Dandelion gave up on herself...

TEN

It was a feeling of warmth that brought Dandelion back from wherever it was her spirit roamed. The kind of warmth she had known as a foal when at dawn her mother wakened her, her warm breath drifting across Dandelion's small back, setting her scrambling to her feet for milk before Daisy left for her day's work.

She wasn't so far gone as to think her mother back at her side, yet, weak and dizzy, in a series of clumsy lurches, she staggered to her feet.

With her senses returning, she had to

blink hard to believe what she saw. Before her stood the oldest, dirtiest horse she had ever beheld. Like a fool she stared at him, her eyes as wavery and unsteady as her legs, wondering if he was really there or if he was a phantom she had brought back with her from a dream.

His coat was white, though here and there through the dirt, mottled dark patches remained to show he had once been dappled gray. His legs were gnarled and bent as though they could scarcely carry his body, and his back was swayed. Whiskers festooned his mouth and chin, and his lips hung loose where teeth had once held them firm.

He was more than old this horse. He was ancient.

"Humph," he snorted, as Dandelion swayed before him. "At least it lives. And who might you be then, lying about out here in the bitter cold as though the life had gone out of you?"

"I... I am Dandelion," she said, her

thoughts as slow and numb as the rest of her. "I... I believe... I think... That is, I think I have lost me way."

"There'll be no arguing with that," he said, his eyes crinkling with mirth, as though her sorry state were a laughing matter.

"And who might you be yourself?" she asked ungraciously, not taking kindly to being seen as a joke.

"What's that?" he asked, leaning close, the better to hear.

Unsteadily Dandelion backed off a pace or two, for he was a frightening old figure seen close.

"Who are you?" she repeated, raising her voice. "And what are you doing here? Are you lost too?"

"Timothy's the name. Tim if you prefer. And no, I'm not lost. Never been lost a day in me life."

"Why are you here then? Have you no master? No place to belong?"

"I did... I did. And a finer man never lived. But he died, God rest his soul."

"Well... Weren't you supposed to stay and work anyway? Didn't someone have a use for you?"

"No. Nobody wanted me. I was too old to their way of thinking to be of use to anyone. But I am to meself! They - me late master's sons - were after having the knacker come put me out of my misery, but a life is meant to be lived to it's end, don't you see, so I wandered off and I'll die natural, in me own time. A long while it is now I've lived free, this being me third winter... Though it may well be me fourth... No matter. A grand life I've had of it from first to last."

Dandelion hung her head at his words. Another one satisfied with his life.

"You're very lucky," she murmured.

His old head came up sharp. "Luck, is it? And why would you be calling me lucky?"

"Why... Because you had a grand life and a good enough master and yet... You seem to be your own master as well."

"Right you are," he agreed with a

satisfied nod. "Indeed and I am. Always was. All me life. Has nothing to do with luck, though."

"But I thought... Well, I always thought that man was the master, and the horse, the slave."

"You did, did you? Well, you've been thinking rubbish. Never mind that now. It's plain to see you're about to expire before me very eyes. Come along with me."

"And where will you be taking me then?"

"Why for food to be sure. Just over this next hill. Food enough for an army there is over there."

"That's a long way," Dandelion told him eyeing the hill. "I don't believe I can do it. Why... It's all I can do to keep meself upright!"

"Sure and you can! Imagine yourself there already and be on your way."

Dandelion was puzzled at his words, not making head nor tail of them and she eyed him dazedly, her face full of questions.

He smiled at her puzzlement and said

again. "It's telling you I am to put a picture in your mind. In that picture see yourself standing at the top of yon hill and then go meet yourself. Sure and that's simple enough, isn't it?"

Dandelion was as confused by his words as she had ever been. They made no sense to her at all and she knew there to be no food on the other side of that hill because she had been there many times. It was as barren and windswept as the one on which they stood. But she didn't have the strength to argue and she was not of a mind to be left alone again. Thinking she might as well die in the attempt as stay where she was, she followed after Timothy's creaking old frame.

The journey up the hill was a hard one for Dandelion with her broken hooves and her legs behaving as if they'd never walked before and all of her senses wavering with starvation.

"There. Now what was I after telling you?" Timothy asked as she came alongside him at the top. "Wasn't it easy then?"

"Easy?" she gasped. "Why, it was more like the death of me, you old fool!"

He gave a long wheezing laugh that rattled his frame at her words, and it was awhile before he had breath to say, "It's easy to see why you got lost, me poor Dandelion. You've never learned the easy way of this world. It's the hard way you've followed all your life. If you'd listened to me back there and used your imagination the way I told you... The way a mind is meant to be used..."

Dandelion didn't hear what he said after that, though she knew his voice droned on. Like a dreamer waking to find he lived his dream, she stared at the small valley that lay before her. Grass, not rock, made up its floor, large clumps of it showing green through the snow.

She was more confused than ever at the sight of it. "So many times I've been this way," she told Timothy through a full mouth. "How is it I never found this place before?"

"You didn't expect to, me poor Dandelion. Firm in your mind you had it that nothing was to be found in these hills but stone and cold and only a tuft of dried grass here and there, so that is all you found. Life is always just, don't you see? It gives precisely what you expect. No more and no less."

Again Dandelion didn't understand his meaning and soon was out of earshot anyway, lured away by ever larger clumps of succulent grass.

It took her a long time to eat her fill. Time in which she wondered at the sudden upturn in her fortunes. In spite of what Timothy said, she thought it lucky that he had found her. Luckier still that he brought her to this sheltered valley high in the hills, safe from huntsmen, and with plenty of food and water besides. "A fine life I can live here," she thought to herself, "and with a companion at me side." A strange one to be sure, with talk that made no sense at all, but better by far than her own sad thoughts.

Strange too, she thought it, that in all her wanderings, she had never seen hide nor hair of this old horse. She, who from her high vantage points, had thought there to be no other living creature for miles around.

Stranger still, in spite of what he said, that she had never found this valley. In mid-mouthful she stopped to think on his words: She hadn't found it because she hadn't expected to? He had to be soft in the head to say such a thing when she had been dying on her feet for the need of just such a place.

"A rare and happy coincidence you should have found me today," she called, approaching him when she'd had her fill and no space left for another bite. "Another day with no food could well have been me last."

"Coincidence?" he asked opening one eye. "Sure and there's no such thing, me darling. It doesn't exist. The world has no place for it. No, there was no coincidence to it at all. I came looking for you. A creature in distress sends out signals for help, don't you see. I knew you were there."

"You mean I was calling out from me dreams?" Dandelion asked, at once amazed and horrified.

"If you're meaning with sounds, no, you weren't. But you were calling out just the same."

"But... How?"

"With your thoughts, me precious. Strong and clear and urgent they were, and meself the nearest to hear."

"You heard me thoughts?

"Now how could I be hearing your thoughts when there's no sound to them? To be sure and I didn't hear them. I sensed them though... Picked them up as it were, with senses of me own. Thoughts travel, me darling, particularly when there's emotion and need at the back of them. A long time it is I've known of your troubles. It was me old bones that could not hurry."

It was difficult for Dandelion to line up her own way of thinking with what he was telling her. She had never heard of such a thing as thoughts going out from her and traveling to others. And if such were the case, why then... the very air about her would be filled, choked, with the thoughts and ideas of others... It was nonsense. Nonsense pure and simple.

Looking at his gaunt, misshapen frame silhouetted against the darkening sky, she wondered if his age and his time alone had twisted his mind as it had his body. And yet... The things he said struck a chord in her, as though he spoke of things she had once known and forgotten. Perhaps then the opposite was true. Perhaps Timothy was very wise indeed.

ELEVEN

Wise he *was*! The wisest creature Dandelion was to ever know, man or beast.

Not that she understood the depths of his wit or wisdom all at once. Often she thought him demented. Other times unkind, cruel even.

In her first days in the valley she hardly knew he was there, being too occupied setting herself to rights as it were. There were her wits to heal with rest and her body with food. But as she grew strong again, she found herself seeking his companionship often, until at the end she plagued him half to death with her everlasting questions. She forgot her first revulsion of his dirty, misshapen body and came to recognize only the essence of him staring out at her through his eyes. They were young, those eyes. And clear. The eyes of youth sunk in an ancient skull.

Of course Dandelion told him the sorry story of her life, it being the only thing she had, or ever would have, that belonged to her alone.

Layer by layer, as soon as she could and as fast as she could, she peeled it back for his inspection, her words coming in torrents as she discovered the luxury of a kindly listener.

Hours it took her and never once did he interrupt. Only his dark, knowing eyes showing that he heard her every word. And when it was all exposed, out there for the two of them to inspect, she sought his approval for all of her actions.

"You do see how it was with me then, don't you?" she asked, anxious for the pity he surely owed her. "Me being neither work horse nor race horse and having Arab blood besides. And being too small for one and without the proper bloodlines for the other... And not belonging anywhere?"

He nodded.

"And that's not the whole of it," she hurried on, urgent by then in her need for sympathy to shine out of his wise eyes. "Now I find I can't live with a master nor yet alone. I am not what I am supposed to be, don't you see? There is no place I belong. I am nothing." At those words she wrenched her own heart so badly she could not go on.

Slowly Timothy shifted his weight from one foot to the other, worrying Dandelion, as he always did, that he would topple in the endeavor, and asked, "And what in the name of all that's holy is it you're thinking you're supposed to be then?"

"Why a work horse," Dandelion said, impatient he had not understood her from the first.

"And did you never, in all this long while, think to see yourself simply as yourself?"

"As meself?"

"Aye. Yourself. Neither work horse nor race horse, just yourself."

"To be sure and I'm meself. Isn't every living thing itself? But I wanted to be more than meself. I wanted to be a race horse!"

"I heard you the first time, me darling. A race horse without a race. And it's wondering, too, I am why you're after setting such limits to yourself, limits that for sure exist only in your own mind and no place itself. Sure and there are a million things you can do in life, as yourself. Is it thinking you are that there are only two alternatives to every little difficulty in the world?"

"I don't think being a misfit all me life and nearly starving to death and having no place on earth to belong are little difficulties," Dandelion retorted, her heart turning cold as the snow at her feet at his lack of understanding.

As if to further bruise her pride, Timothy yawned a great yawn and when he was done with it said, "A sorry tale of woe it is, your life, to be sure and indeed. And tell me, did you never, in all the sad living of it think to make a connection between your thoughts and your actions?"

Dandelion considered his question a long time trying to make sense of it. She made none. In her mind, thoughts were one thing, actions another.

"Let it pass for now then," he said, when she'd opened her mouth half a dozen times to speak and never uttered a word. "Tell me instead," he went on, "what your thoughts are now?"

"Me thoughts?"

"Aye. Your thoughts. What goes around in your head from morning till night? What went on in your head, say, in all the time you were lost?"

"Well... Until I met you, I... I suppose I thought about how hungry I was... How cold... How lonely..." She trailed off, too sad to go on.

"And before that? When you were trying to take your good mother's place. What did you think then?"

"Oh, I was so unhappy," Dandelion sighed, remembering. "I thought no matter how hard I worked or tried to be like her, I would never earn the respect of McCree. And then later, when I stopped trying, I used to worry that he would keep me out in the heat and the cold and the wind and the rain, making me do the same stupid things over and over..."

Timothy nodded, understanding. "And before that?" he encouraged. "When you were with the race horses?"

"Oh," Dandelion brightened. "Why then I thought about how fast I was and of all the races I would win. But... I've told you all this already."

"Never mind. Go on. And before that?"

"Before that? Why, I don't know. I believe I was too young to think at all. I just enjoyed being meself, don't you see? Testing meself. Making up me mind to do a thing one day, executing it the next. I was happiest of all then," she finished softly, "when I was just being meself."

Timothy nodded.

Dandelion laughed bitterly. "Aye, I thought to be meself until I learned me life was planned out ahead of me. Before I knew there existed such things as work horses and race horses." She sighed, "Life was so much simpler then."

"Life is simple, me darling," Timothy said firmly. "It only becomes difficult when you fail to understand that whatever you think about you become. That, and by allowing your head to be filled with the beliefs and opinions of others."

"And how was I after doing that?"

"Well now, you listened to your good mother, may she rest in peace, did you not? And was she not of the opinion that the only good life was the life of the land?"

"Oh yes, indeed. She always said..."

"And your elegant friends, the thoroughbreds? Did they not believe that life, to be valid, had to be lived on the race course?"

"Oh yes, why..."

"And you, me darling, what do you think life is to be lived for?"

Dandelion stamped her hoof at his seeming lack of understanding. "That's just it. I don't know what life is to be lived for. I thought if I were free... That is to say, when I set out on me journey - without ever meaning to, as I told you - I thought then to find the answers in me freedom but now I know that freedom has no answers. A hard thing it is to be free and besides, I am no freer now than I was on the day of me birth. I have not found, in all me travels, the meaning of me life."

"And where will you be looking now, me darling?"

So many questions! He made Dandelion feel like a baby answering to its mother. And what fool questions besides. As if she would go on looking further when she had found in him the answer to all her difficulties.

"I'll not be looking further," she told him quietly. "A grand day it was, the day you found me, Timothy. Not only did you save me life, but a grand new one you gave me besides."

"Did I now?" he replied, his eyes widening in amazement. "And what is this grand new life I'm after giving you?"

"Why the one I'm living now, to be sure. A fine time we'll have of it the two of us. You'll teach me so many things... How to find food and shelter and look after meself. We'll look after each other. Be hermits together..."

She heard him snort and it was a snort of disgust. And she saw pity in his eyes.

"Only the very old are entitled to be hermits," he said, sending a chill of alarm through her body. "The purpose of life is to live it, and there'll be no hiding away from your own here with me."

"But I can't!" she gasped, not believing her ears. "You saw what became of me out there alone. Besides, it's old you are now, Timothy. You'll be needing me just as I need you. Why, the very least I can do is stay with you after all you've done for me! I owe it to you!"

Timothy was scandalized at her words, as close to anger as she was ever to see him.

"I'll not be carrying the burden of your smug self-sacrifice with me to me grave, thank you kindly," he glowered. "Self sacrifice is for weaklings afraid to live their own lives so they foist the responsibility for it on others in the name of kindness. And then expect everlasting gratitude besides! As for owing me, you owe me nothing nor any other creature either! It's yourself you owe. Pay your debts to yourself, little Dandelion! Become the fine horse you were born to be. Make your own contribution! For that is your obligation and that is how you help others, by example. There's no happiness or satisfaction to be found in helping another before you've learned to help yourself. Is it a parasite you're wanting to make of yourself?"

He was calmer then, the humor back in his eyes.

"But I don't want to leave," Dandelion insisted, not caring that he see tears in her eyes. "Why would I? I'm at peace here with you. Safe. Besides... I'd not be staying out of sacrifice at all. I'd be staying because I've come to love you. I want to be with you."

She cringed inside then, fearing that in spite of her terror he would still turn her away.

He did.

With a weary sigh, he said, "No, me darling. You don't love me. You are grateful to me. There's a difference. Love doesn't put the burden of itself on another in the name of gratitude. It doesn't make demands. Love gives... Allows freedom... And asks nothing in return. Come to terms with yourself, little one. Learn to love yourself."

"But Timothy," Dandelion wailed, at her wit's end to make herself understood. "When I'm with you I do love meself. You accept me for what I am, not for what I have or have not become. I am happy with you. Happier than ever before in me life."

"Aye. And I'm telling you again that that is not love. When you love yourself, you won't be needing to see yourself through the eyes of another to feel acceptable. You'll be accepting yourself. Why, what's to become of you if the loved one leaves? Or dies? Will you be chasing off to find another? And then another?"

It had grown dark as they talked but Dandelion's heart was darker still. How cruel he is, she thought. How cold.

"If you make me go away I will surely die," she said quietly, watching his pale outline from the corner of her eye. If she had expected him to come upright at the shock of her words, she was disappointed. If the truth be told, his old head sunk lower, as if her panic were indeed a burden too great for his old frame to support.

"Where would I go?" she asked, her mind such a dark swirl of despair that her stomach churned. "There is no place for me out there."

"Sure and there is," he said. "Every living

thing has its place, else it wouldn't be here. Unless you were so lost in yourself as to be completely blind, you'll have noticed in your travels how often man, in turn, serves his beasts. For whom does he grow his crops and bring in his harvests, if not, in part, for them? A natural give and take to nature there is - a harmony, as it were - where every living thing fulfills its place. From clouds to ants, everything serves everything else, between horse and man, no less than others. There can be equality, each side giving their share. Sure and you know what I'm speaking of. Your good mother and McCree lived it. Did he not love your mother?"

"He didn't love me!" Dandelion burst in hotly.

"To be sure and I know it. Many there are with only so much love in their hearts, and when it is given to one it is gone and none left over for others. So it was with him. You can't be blaming the man. His intentions were good. He did his best for you."

"A poor best it was," she sighed. "A poor

best indeed."

"There's no virtue to be gained in dwelling on past injustices," Timothy said sharply. "McCree is but one man. Millions of others there are, good and bad, and never a-one will you be finding hidden away here. Your place in the world is secure. You must go and find it. Besides, life is not just about finding and learning. There is much for you to teach besides."

"Teach? Me?" Dandelion gasped. "Why, I know nothing."

"You'll teach by being yourself, as we all do. You are the small offspring of two great Clydesdales. Nobler beasts never walked the earth. You are also the descendant of an Arab, the most beautiful and courageous of all breeds. And yet, you are like neither. The world has much to learn watching you become."

"Become? And what is it then that I am to become?"

"To be sure and what else. Yourself!"

TWELVE

Yourself! Yourself! Dandelion's head was spinning at the words. Was there to be no end to it? No quiet little talks. No friendly gossips where he would not be forever forcing her back to herself? He might as well have forced her to look at her own reflection the length of the day, for all the pleasure it gave her.

And yet it was always Dandelion seeking him out and not the reverse. She knew he had the answers to her life and she thought, if she were only clever enough, to wring them out of him.

"This place I'm to be filling..." she began artlessly, coming upon him drinking at a stream. "It's slipped me mind now where it was you said I'd be finding it."

Timothy stopped his drinking to gaze thoughtfully off to the distance, as though searching his mind for the place he had told her.

"I'm not remembering now where it was," he said. "Remind me again where it was you've already searched."

Dandelion was gratified to see her ruse succeed and she half turned her head away for him not to see the satisfaction in her eyes.

"Why everywhere! Far and wide I searched. Uphill and down dale, day in and day out..."

Timothy was thoughtful at that, as though in his mind he saw her, ever searching.

"Ah, yes," he said, "It's remembering now I am and I'm thinking there was one place you didn't think to look."

"Yes? Oh, where? Tell me quickly."

"It's not so much a 'place' I'm thinking

of, for no doubt you noticed in your search that one 'place' is very much like another."

"Why no, I saw no such thing. Some places I found hilly, others flat. I found woods and lakes and..."

"To be sure. All different but, in a way, the same. The only place that is different - unique, you might say - is not to be found out there, but inside."

"Inside? Inside what?"

"Inside yourself."

"Inside meself," Dandelion groaned, but looking down at her chest and along her flanks nevertheless, half expecting, in her bewilderment, to see a signpost invisible until then.

"Yes, inside yourself," Timothy insisted, his wavery old voice grown firm. "Yourself knows where you should be and what you should be doing. You must learn to listen to it, trust it."

"Listen? But to what?"

"To your impulses. Your urges. Your intuitions. They are the part of you that know what is right for you, and they will lead you to your best realization. Listen and you will learn from them."

Memories stirred in Dandelion's mind at his words. Of her earliest days when she had learned to walk, to run. Of when she had trusted herself to do whatever she wanted to do, helped by something that was of her but not of her. The times when she was kept from harm by... She knew not what. The time she had been pushed, almost against her own will, through the gate and away from McCree.

"Is it telling me you are..." she hesitated, "...that there is a part of me that knows what... I do not?"

Even as she spoke, Tim's head was nodding and his smile transformed his face.

"But what is it in me that knows these things?" Dandelion asked.

"Why bless you, me darling, it's the 'you' of you. The soul that began when time began and will go on, long after the 'you' you think of as yourself has gone. Throughout eternity

131

it lives and knows all things as you will, too, when you learn to listen. It is the part of you that chose to be born as you are now. That wanted the challenges such a life would bring."

Dandelion felt a tremble run through her, a prickling in her hide at the thought of so much knowledge and power hidden away inside of herself. But, "How is it then," she asked, "that this clever part of me did not help me these past terrible months when I was so lost and hungry? Or before that? When I was so unhappy working for McCree."

"It was trying, me darling. Always it is there, chattering as it were, prompting you, urging you, eager to help. But you haven't learned to listen. You listened instead to the opinions of others. Opinions that you never thought to question but accepted as fact. You do not have to be so big or so small or fill a certain mold. You only have to be yourself, totally unique, the only Dandelion there ever was or ever will be."

A certain pride Dandelion felt in hearing herself described in such a manner: "Totally unique... One of a kind."

"The beliefs of others it was," Timothy went on, "that stopped you, me poor Dandelion. That made you ugly and resentful. Crippled your spirit. Made you give up. Think, because a handful of beings, out of millions in the world, found you lacking according to their opinions, you gave up on yourself and a terrible thing it was."

And now Dandelion's good feelings were gone, taken away by his words as surely as they were put there by his words. A fool it is, I am, she thought as he spoke. A fool to be sure.

"Turn those beliefs around," Timothy said loudly, bringing her sagging attention back to himself. "Believe that you are special. Believe in your own worth. Find your purpose. Believe in yourself."

"But how...?"

"With beliefs of your own, me darling. And by using the most powerful tool in the universe, your own imagination. Begin by imagining what it is you want to be and know yourself capable of becoming it. Project it forward with emotion. Desire it with all your heart. Then follow the promptings from within and go forward to become your dream! Live it!"

Inspired Dandelion was by his words and she drew herself up tall, felt important, in control of herself and her life.

"And what shall I become?" she asked breathlessly, eager to set off at once in whatever direction he should point out.

"Ask yourself."

"Back to meself again," she glowered, stamping her hoof in vexation. So close had she had him to giving her a direction to follow and he'd trapped her again. "Is that all you'll ever be saying to me then? Ask yourself. Be yourself. Know yourself..."

He grinned his toothless grin. "Aye. Always and forevermore, me darling. For to tell you otherwise is to waste me time and your own as well. True learning only comes from within. To learn elsewhere, from me or others, is to have the knowledge shaded and distorted by the viewpoint of the donor. Can you not see that every time you ask a question of another, you take away from yourself... give a part of yourself away that is rightfully yours... become less instead of more? You know the answers. All of them. They are inside of you and you must listen for them."

"You make me tired," Dandelion said crossly

"Yourself, likewise," he replied dryly, turning away.

"Oh, don't be leaving Timothy. It's sorry I am for me bad manners. Tell me only how to begin and I'll be leaving you in peace."

But Dandelion had pushed him too far and he would not be drawn back. Five words only he had for her, thrown back over his shoulder as he walked away, "Listen to the voice within."

THIRTEEN

"I will then!" Dandelion shouted after him. "See if I don't! I'll show you you're not so almighty clever!"

She saw later she had fallen into his trap, though at the time she was too angry to notice. And if she had, she wouldn't have cared. Timothy could go his own way. She wouldn't be needing him anymore now that she knew there to be a wise, all-knowing part to herself to learn from.

Planting herself firmly with her back towards him, she closed her eyes and settled herself to listen for her instructions.

A long time she waited, all her concentration turned inwards, listening. Many things she heard and felt on the outside of her, but never so much as a whisper from within. She tried changing positions, turning herself first this way, then the other, foolish as it seemed. She stood up and she lay down. She would have stood on her head if she'd known how to do it, so anxious was she to learn the direction of her life.

And, "Timothy," she wailed at the end of it, her new found pride in tatters and not caring if he found her foolish or not. "It's devil a word I've heard this whole long day and me listening me heart out."

"Time," he answered. "Give it time. Remember how it was before when you were very small and obeyed it with never a thought. Easily, naturally. You'll hear it again. Patience."

Patience! How many times Dandelion heard that word from Timothy! So often that the very sound of it had her stamping her hooves in vexation! Many wise and wonderful things she was to learn in her life, but patience came hard to her. Hard, indeed.

"You're trying too hard," Timothy told her at the end of her second day's efforts. "And when you try too hard you get in your own way and then worry sets in. And since worry is a thought just like all others you'll get what you're worrying about and not what you want. You've got to expect it! And by and by, when it's furthest from your mind, you'll hear and you'll know. Go easy..."

"A fine thing it is for you to say 'Go easy'," she told him. "You at the end of a long and satisfying life. But what about me? With me own not yet begun and time wasting."

Nevertheless, she tried feigning indifference and went about her business as though she had not a care in the world, but ready, always, to pounce on the first faint murmurings from within.

But as day followed day, with never a sign, she began to lose her belief in her ability to learn from herself and her head filled up, as before, with the injustices of her past life and feelings of helplessness towards her future.

"Timothy," she said approaching him one dawn after another worrisome night, "it's thinking I am that you've been having me on. Days I've been waiting to hear from me innards the object of me life and never a word have I heard. A hard cold world it is we live in, and I think I must be simple to have listened to a word of your blarney."

"If it's the world you're not liking now, then you'd best change that too," he said, coming slowly out of his sleep. "And before you start pestering me as to the hows of it, I'll tell you. You'll change the world only by changing yourself."

"Is it the whole world you'll be burdening me with now?" she blurted, her eyes stinging with temper.

"Aye, it is. Why would I be putting it on another when it's yourself not satisfied?"

"And where is it you'd have me begin?" she asked, expecting him to say, "Yourself".

Instead he said, "Why any one of a dozen different places I'm thinking. You could stop feeling sorry for yourself as a start."

"Yes, but I have so many reasons..."

"You could start, in a playful way to be sure, to act as if you already led the kind of life you would like to lead."

"But I still don't know what kind of life I'd like to lead."

"You could exercise yourself every day, prepare yourself..."

"Yes, but I've been so downhearted..."

"You could be thinking about what you can do and forget what you can't"

"But I don't know what I can do."

Timothy sighed. Dandelion knew she was trying his patience, but she had her own limits too. The very suggestion that she had to hold herself responsible for her own circumstances and the world besides was really expecting too much.

"You could be making up your mind, now, this minute, just to be a better 'you', than forever asking me questions you can answer yourself."

"Yes, but..."

"Is it thinking you are that if you say, 'Yes, but...' enough times, your life will change all by itself?" Timothy exploded.

Dandelion hung her head at that. "Ah, don't be angry with me, Timothy," she begged. "I want to find the answers meself. It's just that you are so wise and know so much. I think me mother was right. I am just a silly, vain creature. Everything I have ever done turning out badly."

"Everything, me darling Dandelion, is what you think it is, no more and no less. If you will persist in thinking yourself silly, then silly you'll be forevermore."

"And you?" Dandelion asked. "Do you think I'm silly?"

He sighed. "It's not what I think of you nor what others think of you that matter, me darling. It's what you think of you that makes the difference."

Dandelion almost said, "Yes, but..." again, but caught herself in time. Instead, she said, "Timothy, it's knowing I am that you are trying to help me, but you have to understand that all of the things you tell me, about knowing everything meself and using me imagination and having a purpose and... all those things. Well, I never heard tell of the like before and ... ah... well, maybe they are not true at all. Maybe you just think they are."

She thought she might anger him with her words, but Timothy smiled a pleased smile.

"And will you look at who's starting to use her head at last," he said. "Sure and they're true because I think they're true. That is what I've been after telling you all this long time. What I've been telling you from the first. Your thoughts create the 'you' that you think you are, and your whole world besides. That is the purpose of thought, to create, through the imagination. And through emotion! You imagined yourself in great detail, and as you imagined, so you became. You thought yourself fast as any race horse, and so you became. You thought yourself a poor lost soul, dying of starvation and neglect, and so you became. When will you be seeing that everything you ever imagined, you lived? Now, if you don't like the results, change them. Imagine a different you. A you that you will love. Choose!"

"I don't think I could be doing that." Dandelion said uncertainly.

"Sure and I'm telling you, you can! Put a picture in your head of whatever it is you're wanting to become, with all your heart believe yourself capable and worthy, and become it! Isn't that what you did, all unthinking, when you learned to walk? To trot? To gallop? Isn't that what you do when you want to go from here to there? If you had never had a thought in your head, never used your imagination, why, you'd still be lying on the ground where you were born."

"You believe your life now to be the result of your past," he went on, not letting Dandelion get a question in edgewise. "But turn it around, me darling, for the opposite is true. Your life is formed by the thoughts you project into the future. What you think, you become. It's your thoughts going on ahead of you that become your present. You create from the present, not from the past. If you believe yourself a misfit, a poor silly nothing unable to fill any role, then that is what you will become and everyone meeting you will agree with your opinion of yourself. If you expect unfeeling masters and cruelty - ridicule - a harsh, uncaring world, then bless you, you will find just such circumstances, for your thoughts will attract them to you. Thoughts are like magnets, me darling, and always bring you precisely what you expect. Are you understanding now that nothing outside of yourself can harm you? Neither man nor beast. That you are at the mercy of nothing in this world but your own thoughts for they create your life?"

He eyed Dandelion sideways and smiled, no doubt at the variety of emotions chasing one after the other across her face.

She watched him carefully, wondering if

what he said could possibly be true, for if it was, why... anything was possible. And that seemed impossible.

"Is it magic you're after telling me?" she asked doubtfully.

"Nothing magic about it at all," he said sharply, "though there's many that would call it so. Your imagination came with you the same as your nose and your ears. It's your choice which way you use it - to your advantage or disadvantage - the choice is always yours."

"I always thought," Dandelion began and stopped, smiling at her own words. "That is, I always understood there to be a powerful being, not of this earth at all, who created life and put us all here to live our lives as best we can."

"And so there is, me darling, so there is. A powerful being indeed it is. But you're mistaken thinking it not of this earth. Why, bless you, it *is* the earth. And it is every creature that flies or walks or crawls besides. It is what makes eyes see. Hearts beat. Bones grow. Things no mortal can do for themselves. It lives both within and without, this powerful being, a part of everything that is, and not a-way off somewhere distant."

"Does it…" Is it…?" Dandelion shuddered, scarce daring to hope, "Could it be… the part of meself you spoke of earlier? The part that knows all?"

"The very same! What else? And it's wanting for you whatever it is you're wanting for yourself?"

"And why then," Dandelion asked, still not ready to believe him, "since it is all-knowing and wise beyond belief, why doesn't this part of meself help me choose the direction of me life?"

"Because that choice belongs to you. It wants your experience, not its own. Your happiness, not its own. It awaits only your instructions, as it were. Show it, through the pictures in your mind, what it is you want, and it will prompt you, urge you, towards their realization. At birth you are, thereafter you become…"

"Then... If this all-knowing part of me is always with me... Is me... Then... Then I am never alone as I always thought," Dandelion said, her words coming slow. "Nor yet am I a poor lost soul with no part to play in life. Why, this great all-knowing being is... Is Dandelion!"

"Indeed and to be sure! Why the very chain of events that led to you being born into the times you were born, to the parents you were born to, events so complex, going so far back in time, requiring such split-second timing must convince you of that. For no mortal could devise so intricate a pattern. There are no accidents of birth, no coincidences. And how dare you think yourself a victim of circumstance? Why, only a fool would think such a thing. You are here because you chose to be here. Now, what do you choose to become?"

A long time Dandelion stared into those bright young eyes of his. Looking for a joke. Looking for deceit. Looking for truth. They remained as they were. Dark, kind, humorous, studying her as carefully as she studied him.

A dozen times she opened her mouth for another why, another how, and not one did she utter. For now she understood what he had been telling her from the first and she was stunned. At once jubilant and yet terrified of the responsibility implied.

If he was right and she had within herself the power he said she had, and if indeed her thoughts created her life, why then she had only to think, imagine, a better life... No! Why not an amazing, extraordinary life? And live it. But what if she could not control her thoughts? What if, in spite of her best intentions, her old thoughts, the doubts and fears of a lifetime, persisted and kept her prisoner?

So much he gave her to think of, to come to terms with. And so much he took away, too. All her upbringing. Everything she had ever learned and thought she understood. All her ideas of the place of man and beast in a harsh, unjust world. Likewise, the comfort of self-pity, the luxury of blaming circumstance and coincidence and luck, the 'fate' of her forbears. Stripped to her bare bones he left her, cringing, terrified to take on the responsibility of herself.

She felt desolate then, and lonely, cut off from the old Dandelion. She had been comfortable with her, poor thing that she was. And even though she had given endless lip service to her own betterment, never once, in all her chatter, had she thought to take the responsibility of her to herself. Why should she when it belonged elsewhere? To those who bred her... Those who owned her... In the hands of the all-powerful being she had thought apart from herself. "Not to me!" she cried inwardly. "Why, what if I am not gifted with sufficient imagination to create a new life? A new me?"

Not me, she thought again. Not me! I am the misfit. The joke. I am too young still. Too uncertain. Too small. And me head is not right with the rest of me...

She caught sight of Timothy watching her

carefully and she quickly turned away, too overwhelmed even to nod in his direction as she stumbled away to confront herself.

FOURTEEN

To be sure it was herself Dandelion ran from that day, though at the time she thought it was Timothy.

Scarcely able to walk she was, such was her confusion, and she stumbled towards a thicket and hid herself deep in its darkest recesses. A long, long time she stayed there, her mind a battlefield where all her old beliefs fought tooth and nail with Timothy's ideas. Could it be..? Was it possible that one's life was indeed fashioned by thought?

Like a vacant building, she was, its old tenant gone - dead - and its new one loitering at the door, peering through its windows, unwilling to step inside and take up residence, in case the foundation proved false and unable to support it.

She had thought herself alone and abandoned when her mother left her at her birth. And again when she was left to fend for herself in the midst of Lord Harrington's thoroughbreds. And still again when she wandered lost. But never was she more alone than when she plunged herself into that thicket of her own free will. For always before, she had had others to blame for her plight. Now she did not have that comfort, nor ever would again, if what Timothy said was true.

Yet, as time passed, she found her thoughts dwelling more and more on her earliest days, and it seemed to her that, with the innocence of extreme youth, she had indeed lived by her imagination as Timothy said she had. What she had imagined, she had become.

Faint stirrings of pride in her

accomplishments of that period began to pierce through the gloom and despair of her thoughts. Why, she *had* learned more in that year, alone and unhampered by others, than at any other time since. She had gone from a helpless creature not able to stand to a ... Well... It made her smile thinking of how she had been.

So then, if what Timothy said was true and she could create, with her thoughts and imagination, whatever she pleased, what pleased her?

Playfully, shrugging to herself, she tried to imagine what she might become. Nothing came to mind, her entire experience being limited to her previous two alternatives. She dismissed them both. Better to die quickly than put herself between the shafts again. Racing likewise. For she knew at last that she was no more born to race - fast though she might be - than she was born to grow roses. Where then? What then?

The black clouds rolled in again. Imagine it and it is yours, he had said. But imagine what?

A hundred times, a thousand, she thought to exit her shelter and ask Timothy for advice, for direction. And a thousand times she would not.

"Ask yourself," he would wheeze. And ask herself she would though she perish in the exercise.

Endlessly she probed the question, coaxed and cajoled, raked the attics of her mind for a clue, a hint, a suggestion. If you can be anything in the world, what do you choose to be?

I could just be satisfied being meself, as Timothy suggested, she caught herself thinking.

"I am already," she replied. "I want to be more, to grow, to know, to take me place."

"Then be more yourself, start by being proud of yourself."

Now there's an idea, Dandelion thought. I used to be when I was very young.

"Then be proud again!"

"Yes, but... I have nothing to be proud of

at the moment."

"Let's not be going back over that again. Let's try going forward for a change."

"I would, if only I knew where to begin"

"Begin where you are. Alive and breathing on the planet. Young and healthy again. Now... what will you become?"

"If I knew that, do you think I'd be hiding away here?"

"All right, you don't know yet what you are to become, but you could pretend, act as if, you knew."

"And what good would that be doing?"

"All the good in the world. Tell me, if you had already found your place, if you were successful, respected, loved... How might you be feeling?"

"Why... I would feel elated. Proud. Happy!"

"Sure and you would. You'd hold your pretty head high and your steps would not falter."

"Indeed and I would. I would!"

"Well then, there's a picture to hold fast

in your mind. Already you look better, as though you are indeed that horse. Now, create another picture. Imagine a human, someone who is kind and who needs you."

"No. I'll not be having any humans in me life, thank you. I'll not be wanting to be a possession again."

"Don't interrupt! You won't be a possession. We're not thinking of a master. We're thinking more along the lines of a partner."

"And where in the world am I to be finding such a person? If I were to show me face out there again, I'd be trapped, caught, at their mercy again. Thank you again, but no. I'll not be needing any humans in me life."

"You're forgetting a very important thing, Dandelion."

"Am I now? And what might that be?"

"You're forgetting that thoughts are like magnets. That like attracts like..."

"So Timothy said. But I'm not clear in me mind what that has to do with me finding me way."

"It has everything to do with it. You have already imagined yourself a fine horse. Now imagine there *is* someone out there who needs just such a horse as yourself and let your thoughts bring him to you."

"And what would he be needing me for?"

"It doesn't matter, does it?"

"Sure and it matters! He might be wanting me to pull a cart!"

"Do you see yourself pulling a cart again?"

"No! Never..."

"Well, then, he'll not be needing you to pull a cart."

"But what will I be doing?"

"Never mind that for now. Take it for granted, as a given, that it exists and that it's something you will love to do. Something you can do better than any other horse in the world. Something, though, that you could not do without a human."

"But where will I be finding...?"

"It's not important for now. What is

important is that you imagine such a person. Put him alongside the proud 'you' you already carry in your head. He doesn't need a face for now. And now imagine how you would feel if you were just such a horse and there was just such a person and you knew yourself to be living a grand life. Tell me, how does it feel?"

There was a chuckle in Dandelion's throat and joy in her heart as she looked at the picture in her mind. "Why, it's grand I feel! As though I just grew. Stretched. Became powerful. In control of me life."

"Exactly!"

"And is this then how it works, as Timothy was forever saying? You think of a thing. Imagine it. Want it with all your heart... And then it becomes?"

"Sure and it is. Except you forgot something."

"What? Quickly!"

"You forgot the expectation part. You have to expect it. Act as if it has already happened."

"Yes. To be sure. I must expect it. And... who is this then that I am talking to? Is it...? Are you...? Can it be that you're me inner self?"

"The very same! And at your service night and day. Only waiting for me chance to speak."

"And will you...? Are you... always there?"

"How can I be any place else when I am yourself?"

"So simple it is! So, so simple!"

"Indeed..."

Wild with joy was Dandelion, shivering and trembling with it. "Timothy!" she called, leaving her thicket like a fox before hounds. "Timothy, I found it! I found me missing part and I'm through with me antics forevermore. It's a grand horse I am and will be forevermore. Look at me!"

But there was no answering shout. And though Dandelion searched far and wide, high and low, never a trace of him did she find.

In a panic she was to find herself alone again, there still being so many questions to ask, so much still to understand, and she ran about the whole of a day calling to him before she calmed herself and saw his departure for the necessary thing it was.

For certainly with him there, even knowing what she knew, she'd have plagued the life out of him, been after him to do her thinking for her. And she'd have stayed with him, procrastinating, afraid still to set out on a journey of her own devising.

Grieved she was at the loss of him and sore in her heart to know she could never thank him for the grand gift he had given her. The gift of herself to herself. But he was gone. Gone to live whatever future it was he had fashioned for himself in his own mind while he waited for the snows to melt and for Dandelion to come to herself.

And so she returned to her thicket a while longer, there to set about creating, thought by thought, a future tailored precisely for herself.

FIFTEEN

At the magic moment of dawn, the sky palest pink and all else black silhouettes, Dandelion, faithfully following the promptings from within, turned into the long gravel drive that would lead her to Lord Harrington's stable yard. A lot of thought she had given to the most advantageous place from which to launch her grand new life and she knew, despite its proximity to McCree's land and her past humiliations there, that Lord Harrington's estate was the most likely place from which to begin.

Many, many times she had imagined the

moment and now she lived it.

A horse awaited her there at the turn. A beautiful, proud creature it was, lovingly forged in the deepest recesses of Dandelion's mind and sent on ahead to wait for her, its creator, to give it life.

She was fearless, this creation of Dandelion's, with confidence radiating from her in an aura as brilliant as her burnished hide, a creature certain of her worth and jaunty in her eagerness to find and fill her place.

Dandelion's gait changed as the two met, merged. She became her dream and as if in a dream, hooves lilting, moved through the brightening day to meet her future.

Rounding the last curve, she came into the yard and saw what she expected to see, what she had seen on her first visit there long, long ago: tossing, querying heads at each stable's half-door. And all of them amazed at the sight of her, none of them ever having seen, ever dreamed, of a horse unattended by man.

With never a falter in her stride, Dandelion nodded a good morning to each and then, coming to the center of the yard, wheeled about sharply and waited. She was ready and willing at last to take her place alongside man. To become, in her giving and in partnership, more than it was possible to become alone.

Grooms and lads left their work to gawk at the sight of her, none of them knowing what to make of her or what to do with her, and doing nothing until Lord Harrington, together with his assistants, arrived to send them scurrying. In a second a halter was on Dandelion's head and Lord Harrington at her side.

"And what the devil is it we have here?" he demanded of the gawkers.

"Looks to be a runaway, sir," one of the quicker-witted observed.

"A runaway, is it? Well, get it tied up and out of the way then. There's me horses to be attended to. No doubt some vexed owner will be by later to fetch it home."

Thinking the problem of Dandelion dealt with, he turned away to the day's business, only to turn back for a second look at her.

"It's reminded I am of that filly old man McCree - God rest his soul - lost a time back," he said to his veterinarian. "Are you remembering?"

"I am indeed, and I'm thinking you're right though I had to look more than once meself to be sure of it. Wouldn't think it now were it not for the Arab head. Flourished it has wherever it's been. Improved beyond the imagining. A pitiful thing it was in McCree's time."

"That's a strange turn of events then, isn't it?" Lord Harrington mused. "A horse disappears, what...? Must be a year gone. And then turns up here alone, and not a mark on it."

"Aye, strange indeed," the veterinarian agreed. "McCree swore the gypsies made off with it. Said they were welcome besides. Said the horse had a poor disposition and had been a trial to him from its birth. It's trying to remember, I am, what he was after calling it. A flower name, I think it was... Like a daisy, perhaps? No, that was the old mare's name. Wait... It's come to me now. It was a dandelion!"

"Never mind with the name of it," Lord Harrington snapped. "It's more concerned I am with what's to be done with it, McCree being dead and gone and his missus moved away to Dublin." Abruptly he turned away.

"Make inquiries," he called back over his shoulder. "Get the woman's address. Tell her the horse is here."

"And the horse, sir?" a groom asked.

"Put it in a stable for now, out me road. Damnation, half me morning's been wasted on it already. Bring out me horses!"

Overjoyed Dandelion was, to be led off and put in a stable; to see her experience becoming, more or less, the blueprint she had laid out for it. No thought had come to anyone's mind to turn her away, nor had she been labeled one way or another, this leaving all roads open to her, just as she had expected them to be. Moreover, they had seen, remarked on, the change in her. A grand start it was to her plan.

No sooner was she put in a stable than her head was out over the half-door, watching the action from the viewpoint she had coveted from the first. All was chaos until the horses to be exercised formed a ragged line and went off to their morning's work, trailing Lord Harrington and his entourage in their wake.

With the last of them gone and peace restored, Dandelion saw there remained a stranger, a young, slight man she had not noticed before and she watched him closely. He was uncomfortable, ill at ease with his surroundings and himself, and sullen with boredom. His walk was uneven, strange to her eyes, and he steadied himself with a stick.

Aimlessly, trailing his discontent like a dark cloud, he limped from here to there and back again with no more idea of what he did or where he went than a leaf tossed by the wind. He looked into stables not noticing that their occupants were gone. He watched the smithy work without seeing that he formed a shoe. He nodded to lads hurrying by without seeing the faces of any of them. His emotions - bitterness, self-pity, anger - were as clear to Dandelion as the nose on his face and just as familiar. After all, hadn't she'd lived through them all herself.

She nuckered softly to remind him of her presence, and when he looked her way, tossed her head in what she thought to be an encouraging manner.

"Ah, the runaway," he said by way of greeting, "The Dandelion." Slowly he hobbled towards her. The accents of his speech were strange to Dandelion's ears though she would have understood his meaning without words. He spoke in a harsher, more precise manner than the soft brogue she was accustomed to and she learned later that he was from England, a nephew of Lord Harrington's come to recover from the shock of having half his leg blown off in the Great War.

"And where did you run from?" he asked, drawing alongside and reaching up to scratch her head.

Again she nuckered and pawed the half-door, her thoughts going out in welcome.

"A lost horse," he mused. "Well... And aren't we all lost one way or another?"

He frowned at his own words, and a surge of anger and resentment caused him to bring his stick down sharply against his game leg.

"Yes, you might well look startled," he said bitterly as Dandelion stared at his leg, for the sound was not that of wood against flesh but that of wood against wood.

"Wooden legs have a way of sounding strange," he explained. "They feel strange too. Bloody awful, in fact. Be glad you've all your own, though if you hadn't they'd be merciful and shoot you to put you out of your misery."

To comfort him, Dandelion nudged his shoulder with her muzzle as though to say, "Don't be talking so! Sure and you could have lost the both of them!"

"Humph," he grunted and took his leave.

Dandelion was sorry to see him go and she called after him and rattled her stable door with a forefoot to bring him back. She liked the man and wondered if perhaps he might be the one - the faceless one - she had put alongside herself, a vital part to her imagined future.

She had seen him in her mind as very kind, as she sensed this man was underneath his despair, and she'd seen him with a need to grow and change as strong as her own. Her imaginary person would be looking for assistance and she, calling upon all her abilities and her new-found knowledge, would willingly provide it. Not that she had been so foolish as to determine, ahead of time, the specific manner in which the two of them would accomplish their goal, her common-sense knowing it to be something that would evolve and grow out of a combination of shared abilities.

Still, she had not thought to deal with a

man as crippled inside as he was without, as this man plainly was. Perhaps then he wasn't the one. She could only wait and see.

SIXTEEN

Time! Time can be a burdensome thing when one's future hangs in the balance, so to speak.

After all, it's one thing to choose and create in the mind a fine master plan, another to allow the passage of time necessary for it to become physical. The more so when the blueprint calls for others, beside the creator, to fill it out. Because, of course, no scenario can come into being, as it were, without the willing consent of all the players.

Dandelion could imagine Mark - for that was the stranger's name - playing the role she had set aside for a human, with all the fervor of her soul, and not a bit of good would it do her if it did not fit in with the expectations he carried, however haphazard, in his own head.

Powerful indeed is the magnet of the mind, but it can no more attract to it ideas opposed to its own, than a magnet can pick up paper. The attraction has to be mutual.

So Dandelion had to bide her time, and wait to see if Mark was in any way drawn to her, at the same time keeping her mind open - scanning - so to speak, for others who, by their own wishes and desires, might be willing and able to fill her plan. It became then a matter of patience. A quality Dandelion still struggled to master.

Still, there are harder things to learn in life than patience, as Dandelion came to learn in the small paddock she was put into while waiting word from the widow McCree.

There she learned to dodge and fight the doubts that came like gnats to plague her in her long hours of waiting. "After all," they whispered, "for all your fine airs and graces you're still locked behind fences and gates, your life dependent on the whims of humans."

And with the doubts, came their twin, fear. "What if the inner voice was wrong?" it hissed. "And it was a mistake to return to Lord Harrington's. What if Mark sees in you only what the others saw? A runaway. A strange-looking relic of the life of one old, now deceased farmer. And what if Mark decides to leave this place tomorrow and never return? What then, oh, feather-brained dreamer? How long before another kind-hearted stranger comes this way? And what if the good mother McCree instructs your immediate sale? Or your death? What then...? What if... ?"

A grand thing it was that from the start Dandelion had created a fearless, confident mare into whom she had transferred her being for *she* would have nothing to do with the slime of doubt; the degradation of fear. *She* refused to listen to their whisperings and laughed at both of them. Scorned them. Trampled them underfoot with graceful pirouettes where the old Dandelion would have been overwhelmed and left whimpering. The new Dandelion acted as if she already trod the path of her success and reveled in it.

"Sell it!" came word from Dublin, but too late to do Dandelion harm. Too many days had gone by and not one of them had she wasted.

A great fuss she had made of Mark whenever he passed her way, stopping whatever it was she might be doing to rush to the fence and call to him. Her obvious affection amused him, and he took to breaking away from his busy, preoccupied uncle to visit her, a pleased smile at her extravagant welcome on his otherwise gloomy face.

It pleased him, too, that she kept all her attention for him alone, pointedly ignoring the others, grooms and tradespeople from the village, who passed her way. Not for them would she stop her antics to pass the time of day - though they stopped to stare and call out to her - only for Mark.

What antics? Why, the showing-off of every ability she possessed, of course

Like a horse from the famous Spanish Riding School in Vienna she was with her high-stepping, diagonal trot; her controlled canter that kept her almost at a standstill, her pivot from full gallop, the walks she took on her hind legs.

And like a Derby winner she was when, at full speed, she saw corners not as a hindrance, but as a point of acceleration.

And like a horse from the Wild West in her uninhibited bucking that took her from one end of her paddock to the other and across its middle besides.

Oh yes, she showed off shamelessly, but didn't she have to, though? Only herself she had to show, and show herself she did. For how else was she to convince others of her natural abilities, let them know she was more than she appeared to be? Besides, with her new-found self and an audience as well, wasn't she the happiest creature in all of Ireland? Indeed she was.

Well, she's to be forgiven if she was brash. She was young still, only in her fifth year, and convinced at last of her own worth. More than that, she was certain, with each passing day, that Mark saw her as extraordinary. Something to be worked with.

She was right.

"Bring me a saddle," he called to a passing groom one day, when her exhibition had been particularly brilliant.

"The horse has never been ridden, sir," the groom called back. "It's not been broken to the saddle. Used to pull a cart..."

"Bloody ridiculous," Mark fumed. "She's far too good for a cart. It's lucky her spirit wasn't broken in the attempt. She deserves a second chance. She's got to be worth something to someone."

"I wouldn't want to be riding her, sir," the groom said dubiously. "A wild, fiery thing she seems to me, left running loose for a year. And begging your pardon, sir, but you can't be teaching an old horse new tricks."

"I'm not asking you to ride her," Mark said coldly. "As for the other, well, we'll see. Bring out a saddle."

Dandelion forgave the groom thinking Mark a fool for wasting his time. How was he to know she was no ordinary horse, willing to plod through its days thinking itself lucky to put its nose in a feed bag at the end of it?

Like a lamb Dandelion took to a saddle and a bit in her mouth again. Indeed, if Mark had asked for a barn to be put on her back she'd have tried to oblige.

Still and all, she had to be artful. It was one thing to show everyone that she could gracefully and willingly carry a saddle and a rider on her back, quite another to appear so docile and manageable as to be no more challenge to Mark who now had a purpose to his days. As flexible as her blueprint was, there was no room in it for her to be shipped off to Dublin and sold as a riding horse. She still needed to convince Mark that it was he alone who could bring out the best in her.

In that regard, she was helped by her rider, a reluctant jockey with no more desire to school a green horse than ride a goat and who thought himself belittled to be seen on the likes of Dandelion. Together, even with Mark calling out instructions, she made them appear stupid.

"Bring the horse here and I'll show you," Mark exploded at the end of a particularly trying session, the purpose of which had been to teach her to obey commands given by pressure from the rider's legs.

He was exasperated, angry that neither horse nor rider appeared to have made head nor tail of his shouted instructions.

"Get off the horse!" he ordered. "And give me a leg up."

"But, sir. Your leg..."

"Never mind my bloody leg! It's my concern, not yours. I can show you what I mean just as well with one as two. This horse has more to give than you know how to take."

Dandelion was thrilled at those words, knowing her chance to have come at last and knowing herself ready for the challenge.

Mark had the devil's own time getting that wooden leg of his across the saddle, but he couldn't give up. Not with his angry words still ringing in everyone's ears and Lord Harrington, mouth agape, watching from the driveway, he couldn't.

Once on Dandelion's back, he gave no hint of the tumult going on inside him, acting as if he rode and trained horses every day of the week and had all his limbs intact besides. But Dandelion knew his fear, his doubt in his ability to stay in the saddle and live up to his hasty remarks. She felt it in his hands on the reins and in the tension in his body. She knew, too, that while he didn't trust himself, he had no choice but to trust her. So she carried him smoothly, flawlessly, as though carrying crystal goblets on her back. And she obeyed his commands as though they had worked together through a hundred lifetimes.

"...so you see what it is I mean now, don't you?" Mark asked as Dandelion brought him to a smooth halt beside the gaping groom. He spoke in a casual enough manner, but Dandelion knew his face to be tormented with smiles.

"Indeed and I do, sir. It's clear to me now. And tomorrow, when me times me own, I'll be back. A fine horse we'll be making of this Dandelion."

"No need," Mark said airily. "Tomorrow I'll work with her myself."

Mark paid the widow McCree two pounds sterling for Dandelion with the widow thinking herself on the winning end of a bargain!

"A small price to pay for my sanity," Mark would say later, not seeing Dandelion as a possession at all, but rather as an antidote to pain and as necessary to his well-being as he was to hers.

SEVENTEEN

And so they began, a lame man and a mongrel horse, to fashion for themselves a place in the world.

Not that they made a success of it overnight. Far from it. There was teaching and learning to be given and taken on both sides. Battles of will to be won and lost. Abilities to be gauged and worked with, and strengths and weaknesses to be defined.

They were two novices. One putting himself back together without the benefit of a Timothy. The other, untrained, blundering, but filled with such an eager willingness to learn that she pushed Mark to accomplish things he had never thought to do again.

It was a time of sweat and frustration. And a time of joy and achievement in seeing a dream become real.

There were hours and days when it was Dandelion, not understanding what Mark wanted of her, that stretched his patience beyond the breaking point. Other times it was him, struggling with the dual handicap of a missing limb and a lack of confidence, that had Dandelion at the end of her wits, nudging and cajoling, pestering, until he put a saddle on her back and tried one more time.

They came a long way that summer, the two of them. The runaway became a sleek, perfectly schooled mount; the cripple, a horseman again, his bitterness forgotten, his spirit healed. People forgot that Dandelion had ever been McCree's runt and thought of her only as Mark's horse.

In no time at all Dandelion earned a stable of her own, her name in brass above its door, and a groom to see to her every need. Under his brushes her coat acquired a sleek gloss that would have blinded McCree, and her mane and tail were untangled and trimmed so they flowed like fine silk. She saw the last of her hand-me-down harness with the arrival of her own saddle and bridle from Dublin, and she was enchanted at the clatter she made stamping about the cobblestone yard in her new-forged shoes.

Oh, but it was grand to be pampered and respected! To kick at her stable door along with the rest of them and have her shrill demands attended to on the double. Just so she was fed, her diet overseen by the veterinarian. And just so she was watered, never being allowed to drink her fill after exercise until her body had cooled. And just so her life would have continued, in ease and luxury, had she not become bored and dissatisfied, even though she knew this made her appear ungrateful.

But not nearly enough of a life was it for her to be on the sidelines of the rarefied world of racing that swirled about her yet did not take her in. Not satisfying enough, either, were the morning lessons, which only polished what she already knew, nor the long treks through the countryside in the afternoons. She felt herself only half alive. She wanted to be a leading lady, not a bit player, or worse, a pet.

After all, in the grand plan she had so carefully imagined in the valley, she had seen herself living in a manner that challenged her every thought, her every ability... And she was impatient for that part of her dream.

In Mark too, there was a growing restlessness, a need to leave behind the comfort and ease of his uncle's estate and find for himself a place in the post-war world. He was far too young to live without a challenge or a purpose. And yet, what could he do?

Moodily, he considered possibilities. He would work for his uncle... He would start a business of his own... He would take a desk job with the war office... He would teach riding... He would open an Inn...

And moodily, he rejected them all knowing none of them would give him what he missed most from his military days: the camaraderie, the competition, the travel, the horses, the discipline...

"I'll go mad if I stay here much longer," he told Dandelion on one of their afternoon rides. "There has to be something out there for me. But what? Where?"

Dandelion was uneasy at his words. What was to become of her if he found what he was looking for? Would he leave her behind? Angrily she pushed these fears out of her mind remembering Tim's words, "...worry is a thought just like all others and you *will* get what you think about." She couldn't afford to think such things. She'd come too far. Resolutely, she put back in her mind, the image of herself with Mark, both of them challenged and excited by the life they led. But what was that life to be? If only she knew more of the ways of the world...

And then one day, by what she knew better than to call a coincidence, the direction for their future came to find them.

It happened that a friend from Mark's old regiment was in the district and came to see him. Mark took him out to the stables to show him Dandelion.

"What an extraordinary looking animal," the friend, David, said trying to hide a smile. "What on earth breed is it?"

"It is an extraordinary animal," Mark said cooly, ignoring the question. "Ride her. You'll see."

"My dear chap," David said hastily, "I wouldn't dream..."

"Oh, but you must," Mark said, quickly strapping on Dandelion's bridle and saddle and leading her out of the stable, "I insist. She's a wonderful ride."

Reluctantly David mounted and rode Dandelion out to the paddock where he half-heartedly put her through her paces. "Very nice," he said bringing Dandelion back to the gate where Mark waited. "You've schooled her well. She responds beautifully." He dismounted.

"Oh, come on!" Mark said. "You haven't seen the half of it. A riding school hack could do what you just put her through. She can do much more than that. Here, I'll show you," and he swung into the saddle.

"I believe you, old chap" David said. "There's really no need for an exhibition. And, I say, it is a bit chilly out here..."

But Mark wasn't listening. It annoyed him that the hard work he and Dandelion had put in, the only work he had been capable of doing for so many months, should be taken so lightly.

Sensing Mark's determination to show not only what an outstanding mount he had made of her, but also how well he had overcome his missing leg, Dandelion was on her mettle, all her attention focused on his every command, and for over half an hour they went through their most daring and complex exercises.

David clapped as they finished with a flourish beside him.

"You were right!" he enthused. "My God!

She's brilliant! And who would ever think it, looking at her. I mean, she is..." he faltered seeing Mark's smile turn to a scowl. "I mean, well... one wouldn't expect so much talent in such a... uh..."

"Never mind what she looks like," Mark said crossly, "it's what she can do that matters."

"You're quite right," David said, "And there's a lesson for all of us in that. I'm sorry. Anyway, I was just thinking, I know a chap who'd buy her in a minute if I brought him out here and you showed him what she can do."

Dandelion's heart almost stopped beating at those words. But only for a moment. Mark's reply was exactly what she would have liked to say herself.

"She's not for sale," he said, his voice so cold and hard Dandelion hardly recognized it. "But," his tone lightened, "out of curiosity, what would this chap of yours want with her?

"Well, actually, he's scouting for polo ponies. Wants only the best. Willing to pay top price. Big demand for them now the war's over, you know. I should think with her intelligence you could have her trained in a fortnight or so. Why don't I have the chap come by and take a look at her, just in case you change your mind..."

But Mark wasn't listening. At the word polo his eyes had narrowed. "Polo," he muttered. "My God, of course. Polo!" He smacked his forehead. "Why didn't I think of that? All this time puttering around here wondering what on earth to do next and the answer's been staring me in the face. It's so obvious. She's perfect for it. It's the very thing for her. For both of us. I could... That is, we could... And as for my leg... Well, what of it? With Dandelion to see me through, no one need ever know. It's brilliant. The very thing..."

"I'll have the chap get in touch then, shall I?" David said, "...set up an appointment to come and have a look at her."

"Not bloody likely," Mark snapped. "I'll train her myself! And I'll ride her myself!"

"My dear chap, be reasonable," David said condescendingly, "I mean, I know you've worked wonders with those injuries of yours, but after all... Polo? It's grueling. You could never do it. What rotten luck, eh? I mean, you were so awfully good at it. I remember seeing you play before the war..."

"You're as bad as the rest of them," Mark exploded. "God, if I'd listened to all of them I'd still be in a wheelchair. And I certainly would have never ridden again. No, tell your chap he'll have to look elsewhere. I've made up my mind. Dandelion and I will do it together. It's settled. Come along now, let's get you in front of a fire. You're turning blue with the cold. We'll have a drink together... Celebrate... I mean, really I can't thank you enough. You've given me the key to my future! And Dandelion's too! If you only knew how I've been wracking my brains."

* * *

It was as if Mark had opened a magic door to Dandelion the day he first brought out his mallet and began teaching her the intricacies of the game of Polo. A door that never closed as long as she lived.

Seeing her in the thick of a match, many believed that Dandelion was born and raised to the game, so precisely did its requirements match her attributes. For a polo pony has to be large enough to carry a grown man at great speed and yet, at the same time, it has to be small enough to turn quickly, handily, without getting in its own way. And what better size than Dandelion?

And a polo pony needs great wit and spirit of its own, yet an obedient, willing temperament to respond instantly to its rider's commands. And who better than Dandelion with her fine Arab blood and Mark's inspired training?

And it needs legs of iron to gallop miles of an afternoon on the hard ground of the field. And great muscular control to stop and turn from a full gallop. And who better than Dandelion with her Clydesdale heritage and McCree's great stone walls barring her early development?

Most of all, a polo pony needs a strong imagination of its own. And who knew more of that than Dandelion?

Like a child at its first Christmas Dandelion remained all her life at the sight of a polo field, the sound of the ball on wood. For polo caught her imagination and held it fast ever after. In it she found everything she needed to fill and become the second part of the fantasy she had created in her mind. In it she found the challenge she had sought, the freedom to be herself, the purpose of her life. In it she took center stage and became the brilliant being she had imagined herself to be. And in all the world and throughout all time, there will never be another quite like her.

The End

EPILOGUE

Legends grow up around every sport. They have around polo. In all parts of the world where the game is played, when the matches are over and the players gather to replay every point at their leisure over drinks and dinner, talk will often shift to other games in other times and other places. When it does, those who have been around the sport a very long time remember Dandelion, the misnamed chestnut with the head of an Arab and Mark, the one-legged horseman who brought her to the attention of the world.

Conversation will not dwell long on the victories they scored; victories that span continents and are well documented in yellowing sporting pages, in silver trophies locked away behind glass doors, and in photographs where Dandelion's spectacularly beautiful head jumps out of every crowd. For none of these can begin to convey what it had been like to see them together and sense the extraordinary understanding that existed between them in the heat of play.

As though, they said, when the game began, there ceased to be a horse and rider altogether, but rather, that the two became one, an indivisible entity unto itself - like the centaur of legend - with one mind, invincible in its superior power and intelligence.

No one was ever quite sure where Dandelion came from, though many, wanting to know the secret of her breeding, asked.

"She's one of a kind," Mark always answered vaguely. And so they thought, assumed, that he had brought her back from India when his regiment returned home. Anyway, for their purposes, the saga of

Dandelion began at the end of the Great War, in 1919 or thereabouts, and lasted until 1939 when she died, as great a legend in her time, as her ancestor, the magnificent Almustaq, had been in his.

"Amazing little thing she was that Dandelion," someone will begin, and the room will fall silent, the listeners avid to hear more of the legend. "Remember seeing her at Windsor..." (They could just as well have said Cowdrey or any of the other fields stretching half way around the world where Dandelion had played the game.) "Never saw anything like her in my life. Knew the game better than a human if you ask me. Played each chukker as though she knew, ahead of time, the game plan. As though she had seen it played already and knew exactly where she had to be every second of it. Knew the run of the ball before the damned thing was struck! Knew how far it would go too and had herself there ahead of it, at the precise distance the chap needed to make his swing! Oh, she was clever! And brave!

She'd have herself in and out of melees that would have daunted angels. Amazing! Never seemed to tire. Had the stamina of a horse twice her size. Never went lame either. Always had the same enthusiasm from first to last..."

"Fancied herself, too!" another speaker will take up where the first left off. "She'd come out onto the field at the start of a game as though she led an army to war, as though she danced to music the rest of us couldn't hear. She'd have that beautiful little head of hers tucked tight into her neck, ears pointing straight forward, hooves lilting, tail bannered. Thought herself the Great Horse of Troy, I always said. But once the signal for play was given, look out! She was a different horse then, by Jove! A red-gold blur! Couldn't keep track of her she moved so fast from one end of the field to another. Never saw a horse stop so fast nor turn so sharp either. Don't expect to ever again..."

"The chap turned down fortunes for her," someone else will go on, slowly turning brandy in a glass. "Offered to buy her myself more than once, even though she was well past her prime. He laughed at me! Said there wasn't enough money in the world. Damn right, too! How could you put a price on her? She was unique. A legend. And legends don't come with price tags."

Creed of a Dandelion

Picture in your mind
All that you may be
And with a little time
You will come to see:
That in the game of life
Your dreams will come alive
By thinking of the end result
As if it had arrived.

Michael Dooley

About the Author

Sheelagh Mawe was born in Hertfordshire, England where her passion for horses was equaled only by her love of reading. Later, as an adult living in America and inspired by various metaphysical authors, she decided to put their theories into story form, using a horse as her protagonist. Sheelagh now lives in Orlando, Florida where, together with two of her three adult children, she helped found Totally Unique Thoughts, an inspirational gift company. She is presently working on several new books and screenplay adaptations.

DANDELION

Makes a Wonderful Gift!

To order more copies go to her web site at:

www.tut.com/Dandelion.htm

Or you can order through your local bookstore.

All Totally Unique Thoughts books may be purchased
for Educational, Business, or Sales Promotional use.
For information please write:
Special Markets Department
Totally Unique Thoughts
P.O. Box 2962
Winderemere, Fl 34786-2962